The Bed That Ran Away

and

Other Stories

by

ENID BLYTON

Illustrated by
Lesley Smith

AWARD PUBLICATIONS LIMITED

For further information on Enid Blyton please contact
www.blyton.com

ISBN 1-84135-009-5

This compilation text copyright © 2000 The Enid Blyton Company
Illustrations copyright © 2000 Award Publications Limited

Enid Blyton's signature is a trademark of
The Enid Blyton Company

This edition entitled *The Bed That Ran Away and Other Stories*
published by permission of The Enid Blyton Company

This edition first published 2000
5th impression 2003

Published by Award Publications Limited,
27 Longford Street, London NW1 3DZ

Printed in Singapore

CONTENTS

Five Naughty Lambs

Robbie got up very early one morning. It was exam day at school, and Robbie hoped to get top marks in Nature. That meant a prize, and the prize was something lovely – a camera!

Robbie was very good at Nature. He knew a great many birds, almost all the flowers that grew in the fields around, and could tell you at a glance the name of any tree you asked him. He did badly want to win the camera, and as he was far and away the best boy at Nature, he was quite certain he would. That was why he was up early – just to make sure of a few things he had learned that term. He sat huddled up in a chair, looking through his books carefully to see if there was anything he had forgotten.

But there wasn't. Robbie was pleased. He was quite ready for his breakfast when his mother called him. He sat at the table and ate porridge and then an egg, and toast and marmalade. Then he got himself ready and started off in good time for school. The Nature exam was the first one that morning, so he wanted to be early.

He had a long way to walk to school, over the fields, down lanes and over the common, but he didn't mind. He could see plenty of birds and flowers on the way and he liked that. It was early in the spring now, and the primroses were just beginning to show in the ditches.

By the Long Meadow there was a sloping field in which sheep and lambs were kept. Robbie always looked over the gate as he passed for he liked to see the lambs skipping about and wriggling their funny long tails. This morning he looked over the gate – but he couldn't see the five little lambs anywhere in the field!

The sheep were there. Robbie counted

them to see if they were all there. Yes –
there were fifteen of them as usual. But
where were the five little lambs?

Then he saw them. They were at the
top end of the sloping field, trying to get
through a hole in the hedge there!

"Good gracious!" said Robbie. "If they
get through there they will be on the
main road, and will be knocked down by
a car. Whatever shall I do?"

He stood and watched for a minute or two, hoping that the naughty little lambs would find it too difficult to squeeze through the hole – but to his dismay he saw first one, and then another, and then the rest of them slip easily through the gap out on to the road beyond. Robbie could hear the hum of cars going along the road there.

He didn't know what to do. The farm was a good way away, and by the time he got there to tell the farmer what he had seen, the lambs might be knocked down and hurt. But if he ran across the field and tried to get the lambs back again he would be terribly late for school. And then he would miss the Nature exam!

"Oh, well, it's no business of mine," said Robbie, aloud. "I expect someone will see the lambs on the road and shoo them back into the field. They'll be all right."

He turned to go – but as he went he saw in his mind those five little lambs. Suppose, just suppose, a car knocked them down, and broke their little skippitty legs! It would be dreadful.

"I couldn't bear it," said Robbie, and he turned back to the gate. "It's no good saying it isn't any business of mine. It *is* my business. I shall miss the Nature exam, I expect, and I shan't get that camera. Oh dear! Perhaps I can get the lambs back to the field quickly, then run all the way to school and be just in time."

He climbed over the gate and rushed at top speed up the sloping field. Out of breath and panting, he reached the gap

where the lambs had squeezed through. He slipped through it himself and looked up and down the road for the lambs.

They had gone such a long way! Robbie ran after them, and when he was nearly up to them a car came by. The driver didn't see the lambs, and was almost on top of them when one ran right in front. Robbie yelled loudly and the driver put on his brakes. The car stopped just behind the frightened lamb.

"Hey!" shouted the driver, crossly, thinking that the lambs belonged to Robbie. "What are you thinking about, you silly boy, letting your lambs run about in front of cars like this! You ought to know better."

Robbie was just going to explain that they were not his when the driver drove off. The little boy was almost in tears. It was bad enough to have to go after the lambs on exam morning, but even worse to be scolded for something that wasn't his fault!

The lambs rushed on. Robbie ran behind them, trying his hardest to get

in front so that he could drive them back. At last he managed it. Back they all went, and in five minutes' time Robbie was shooing them through the field. Then he looked at the gap in the hedge and thought hard.

"They will get out again, as sure as anything!" he said. "I'd better quickly block up the hole."

He broke off a few branches from a hawthorn tree nearby and blocked up the gap. Just as he was finishing a car came up behind him and stopped.

"What are you doing there?" roared an angry voice. Robbie turned round. It was the farmer!

He thought that Robbie was trying to make a hole through the hedge. He hadn't seen that the little boy was trying to mend the gap.

"Oh, please, Mr Brown, your five lambs got out into the road and one was nearly run over," said Robbie. "I saw them from the gate down there as I was on my way to school. So I came up and got them back, and now I am just filling up the hole so that they can't get out again."

"That's very kind and helpful of you," said the farmer. "Those lambs might have been killed. I'm much obliged to you."

"What is the time, please?" asked Robbie.

"Twenty minutes past nine," said the farmer, looking at his watch.

"Oh, goodness!" Robbie said in dismay. "School begins at nine o'clock! The Nature exam is at half past. I shall miss it."

"Well, you won't mind missing an exam, will you?" said the farmer in surprise. "I hated exams when I was a boy. Come along, you can hop into my car. I'm going past the school and I'll drop you there."

Robbie climbed in. He was very disappointed. Even with the lift in the car he wouldn't be in time. He would miss the exam and wouldn't get top marks after all.

Robbie didn't cry, for he was a brave boy – but he couldn't say a word more. He just sat in the car looking straight in front of him. Mr Brown wondered what was the matter. He looked once or twice at Robbie and he looked so disappointed and miserable that he asked him what the matter was.

"Well, it's like this," said Robbie. "You see, Nature is my best subject and I meant to get top marks and win the prize. It's a lovely little camera. Now I shan't be in time for the exam, so I shan't get top marks or win the camera. I'm just a bit disappointed, that's all."

"I see," Mr Brown said thoughtfully. "That's bad luck."

He drove on and at last came to the school and Robbie got out. But, instead of going on, the farmer got out of the car himself and went in through the school gates. He walked up to the front door, rang the bell, and asked to see the headmaster.

Robbie ran round to the cloakroom to hang up his coat. No one was there. Everything was silent. He had seen all the boys and girls sitting in their classroom, writing their exam papers.

The cloakroom door opened and the headmaster looked in. Robbie was afraid he was going to be scolded.

"Please sir," he began – but the headmaster stopped him.

"All right, Robbie," he said, with a smile. "I know all about it! I've heard about the lambs, and Mr Brown seems very grateful to you. He has asked me if you can take the Nature exam with the others, although you are late. Of course you can – you can easily have twenty minutes over the time, when the others have finished, to make up for the time you have missed. Hurry along now, and take your pencil box with you. I will explain things to Miss Harrison, your teacher."

Well! Robbie could hardly believe his ears! So he was going to take the Nature exam after all! He rushed off to his school room and was soon sitting down in his place. Miss Harrison gave him the Nature paper and he looked at it. He could answer all the questions perfectly! It was a lovely exam.

And when Prize-giving Day came, and all the exam marks were read out, who was top in the Nature exam? Yes, Robbie, of course! He got the camera – and then he got a big surprise!

"There is a special prize given this term by Mr Brown for kindness to animals," said the headmaster. "And he wishes it to be given to Robbie Hill for saving five of his lambs from being knocked down in the road. I am very glad that Robbie is to have it. Robbie, come and collect it."

Up went Robbie to the platform, as red as a beetroot with delight. And what do you suppose the prize was? Guess! A black spaniel puppy! What do you think of that? Robbie was so surprised and delighted that he could hardly say thank you. But the puppy said it for him – "Wuff!" it said, "Wuff! Wuff!"

"What a good thing I went after those five naughty lambs that morning!" thought Robbie as he went back to his seat. And it certainly was, wasn't it?

The Story of Twiddle and His Cure

Once upon a time there was a pixie called Twiddle. He lived in the village of Kind-Heart, so you can easily guess what the people were like there.

They were very kind indeed. They gave each other lots of things, they worked for each other, and they loved each other. Twiddle should have been a happy little pixie to live in such a nice place – but he wasn't.

He lived in his tiny cottage with his aunt, Dame Twinkle. She looked after him, and did everything she could to make him happy. In fact, she did so much for him that she made him very lazy.

A day came when Twiddle wouldn't even carry the logs in for Dame Twinkle. He said he was too tired, she must do

them herself. The old dame puffed and panted, but she brought in all the logs, and then asked Twiddle if she should make him a nice hot cup of cocoa, to cheer him up a bit. Wasn't it kind of her?

Twiddle got worse and worse. When village folk brought him presents of honey and new cakes, fresh-picked apples or fine balloons, he took them, and hardly said "Thank you." He didn't ask if he could do anything in return, and even when his big pear-tree was simply loaded with fruit, he wouldn't let Dame Twinkle give a single pear away!

He was growing very selfish, and very lazy. He knew he was too, but he didn't bother. Then one day his cousin from Blackberry Wood came to tea with him.

"Twiddle, you're getting fat and pasty," he said. "Also, I notice that you haven't offered me anything but bread and butter to eat. There is no jam on the table, and not a single cake. Is this the way to treat your own cousin? Something horrid has happened to you. I believe – yes, I really do believe – you are getting mean and selfish! And, you know, you oughtn't to live in Kind-Heart village if you're unkind. If the Fairy Queen got to hear of it, she would be very cross, and would turn you out."

Twiddle listened in dismay. Yes, he knew he was a mean and selfish pixie, he knew he was lazy and unkind – but dear me, he couldn't bear the thought of being turned out of his own village! What a disgrace! Then he thought of a good excuse.

"It's you who are unkind!" he said. "I'm not feeling well, that's what's the matter with me! I'm a poor, ill pixie, and you oughtn't to talk to me like that!"

"Poor darling Twiddle," said Dame Twinkle, coming in just as he spoke. "Is your cousin being horrid to you? He had better go, then."

"I'm not being horrid to him, I'm just telling him the truth," said the cousin. "If he's as ill as all that, why doesn't he go and ask the doctor to put him right?"

"I don't want a doctor," said Twiddle, in a hurry. "I may get better soon."

But Dame Twinkle was very much worried about her darling Twiddle. She had really believed him when she had heard him say he was ill. So, without saying anything to him, she went out to Doctor Hey-Ho's and begged him to call and see Twiddle.

"What's the matter with him?" asked

the doctor. "I saw him going by yesterday, and he looked all right."

"He's quite altered lately," said Dame Twinkle. "He's too ill even to carry in the logs every day for me, Doctor."

"What!" said Doctor Hey-Ho. "Does he make you carry them, then? The naughty little pixie!"

"Oh, no, he's not naughty," said Dame Twinkle. "He's just ill, Doctor. Why, he never does anything for anybody, even when they bring him presents of honey and new-made cakes. I'm sure he's not strong enough. Sometimes he can't even do up his own shoes, so I have to do them for him."

"Oho!" said the doctor, in a funny sort of voice. "Yes, he certainly sounds as if he has something strange the matter with him. I'll call in and see him tomorrow."

So he came the next day, and Twiddle was surprised and cross to see him.

"I've come to see what's wrong with you," said Doctor Hey-Ho. "Put out your tongue, say 'ninety-nine' three times, and cough."

Twiddle did as he was told. Then Doctor Hey-Ho felt his pulse, punched him in the chest, pinched him in the legs, shook him by the shoulders, and then sat him down very hard on a chair.

"You're dreadfully ill!" he said solemnly. "You must come with me, and be cured."

Twiddle was frightened. He didn't really feel ill. He was only just lazy and mean, but he didn't care to say that. What was he to do?

"I don't want to leave my village," he said. "I shall stay here with my Aunt Twinkle. She can look after me if I'm ill."

"I can't allow that," said Doctor Hey-Ho, in a very firm voice. "What you've got is catching, and your aunt might get ill, too, and your neighbours. You must come home with me."

So there was nothing for it but for Twiddle to go home with the doctor. He cried, but it was no use. The doctor was very firm, and though Dame Twinkle begged to go with them so that she might look after Twiddle, he wouldn't let her.

Twiddle packed up a few things, and was soon ready. He was very cross, but Doctor Hey-Ho took no notice. He just held him tightly by the hand, and marched him off to his house, which lay some way outside the village of Kind-Heart.

When he got there, he showed Twiddle a tiny bedroom with a hard little bed in it. "This is yours," he said. "Unpack your things, and then come and get supper for me."

Twiddle stared, but Doctor Hey-Ho had gone. Get supper indeed! Wasn't he ill, and needing to be waited on and looked after? What did that nasty old doctor mean?

He unpacked quickly, and then ran into the other room. The doctor was sitting down and cleaning some of the things out of his bag.

"Bread and milk for supper," he said. "The things are all in that cupboard. Hurry up, I'm hungry."

"I'm not going to get supper," said

Twiddle. "I came here to be cured of my
illness, not to make myself worse."

The doctor smiled very broadly.

"This is part of your cure," he said.
"You'll soon feel much better! Now then
– out with those supper things, or you'll
have no supper!"

Twiddle said no more. He was frightened, for he had heard that Doctor Hey-Ho was very good at spanking people if they disobeyed him. He got out the supper things, and made the bread and milk. He put the bigger bowl for himself and the smaller one for the doctor.

"You're more ill than I thought," said the doctor, looking at the two bowls. "You'd better not have any bread and milk tonight at all. It wouldn't be good for you."

He ate both bowlfuls himself, and Twiddle had to go to bed hungry. He made up his mind to give the doctor the bigger bowl the next time – so you see he was already getting a little better!

Next morning he lay in bed hoping that Doctor Hey-Ho would bring him his breakfast. But nobody came at all. Eight o'clock struck, and then nine o'clock, and then ten. Still the lazy pixie lay in bed, waiting. But at last, hearing no noise in the other room, and feeling very hungry indeed, he jumped out of bed and dressed.

When he went into the kitchen, there was no one there. The fire was out, there was no meal on the table, and everywhere looked dusty and dirty. The pixie felt very cross. Then suddenly he saw a note pinned to the mantelpiece.

To the Pixie, it said.

Twiddle read it all through. This is what the doctor had written:

I have had to go and see someone who is very ill. Please lay the fire and light it. Then boil an egg for your breakfast. Then go to the woods and bring in more firewood, for there is not much left. After that sweep and dust the rooms. Then cook a nice lunch for me.

You should feel very much better after doing all these things.

Doctor Hey-Ho.

Twiddle couldn't believe his eyes. What, was he really to do all that hard work? Well, he just wasn't going to, then! He sat down on a chair and sulked for five minutes. Then he suddenly felt so dreadfully hungry that he couldn't bear it any longer. He really must have some breakfast.

To boil an egg, he had to make a fire. So he got the firewood, and lit a fine fire. Then he boiled a kettle for some tea, and cooked himself a nice brown egg. After that, he felt much better.

"I might as well do a bit of dusting and sweeping," he thought. "There's nothing else to do – besides, the doctor would be sure to scold me if I didn't obey him. Oh, dear, I do wish he hadn't brought me here!"

He went to the mantelpiece and read the note again. He saw that he had to go to the woods for some firewood, so he put on his muffler and out he went. He soon reached the woods, and began looking for firewood.

In a short time he had a big bundle tied together and, puffing and panting, he carried it to the doctor's.

"Logs would be much heavier," he thought. "I'm glad I didn't have to carry bundles of logs."

Then he remembered how his old aunt Twinkle carried logs every day for him, and for the first time he felt ashamed and sorry.

He stacked the wood in the shed, and then went to read the note again. He next took a broom and began to sweep. Then he dusted, but by this time he was rather bored, and he didn't do it very well. He didn't think the doctor would notice the corners he had missed.

By this time it was half-past twelve, so he thought he had better cook something for Doctor Hey-Ho's lunch. He had only just begun when the doctor rushed in.

"What, no lunch ready?" he cried. "And do you call this dusting? Why, look at the dirt in that corner! I can see you had better have a spanking, Twiddle. I'm sure that would make you feel much better!"

"No, it won't really," said Twiddle.

"Please, Doctor, I'll do all the dusting
again this afternoon. I'm very sorry, I'm
afraid I was lazy."

"Hm!" said Doctor Hey-Ho, looking at
the pixie. "Well, we'll see. You look a bit
better, I must say."

Lunch was soon ready, and the two ate
a good meal. Then the doctor rushed out
again, telling Twiddle to have his tea
ready at four o'clock.

How hard Twiddle worked that

33

afternoon! He swept the rooms all over again, and dusted them carefully. Then he cleaned the windows. After that he made some toast, and boiled the water for tea. When Doctor Hey-Ho came in, the table was set by the fire and everything was ready.

"You're getting better," said Doctor Hey-Ho, looking round the room. "I said you'd soon be cured, Twiddle. A few weeks of this, and you'll feel quite a new pixie!"

Twiddle nearly dropped his piece of buttered toast when he heard that! A few weeks! How dreadful! But he dared not say anything, so he just went on eating his tea.

That evening Twiddle was sent out with medicine to deliver. It had been pouring with rain, and there were puddles everywhere. The poor little pixie fell into ever so many, and got wet through. He cried with rage, and when he got home again, he told the doctor that he would really be very ill indeed if he had to go out in the wet like that.

"Nonsense!" said Doctor Hey-Ho. "Change your shoes and stockings, and drink some hot milk. You'll be as right as rain!"

The funny thing was that after Twiddle had got his feet warm and dry, and sat by the fire drinking a nice cup of hot milk, he felt quite cheerful and happy. He told the doctor about all the puddles he had fallen into, and the doctor laughed heartily. Twiddle thought it was a good joke, too, and he went to bed in a very good temper.

The next day he worked for the doctor, and got the meals as before. But this time he whistled as he worked, and forgot to frown and scowl. That night he delivered medicine again, and stopped to hear the people talk about Doctor Hey-Ho.

"Oh, he's a wonderfully kind man!" they said. "He's so unselfish and so hard-working. He'd do anything for anybody, would Doctor Hey-Ho!"

Twiddle listened, and thought a lot. He wished people would love him as they

loved the doctor. He wished the doctor would like him, and tell him he was a good worker. But Doctor Hey-Ho said never a word of praise.

Twiddle worked very, very hard all that week. He made the little house spotless, and everything shone like silver and gold. He cooked delicious meals for the doctor, and cheerfully delivered all the medicine every night.

And, dear me, he felt quite a different person! He wanted to smile and he wanted to make jokes. He wanted to carry parcels for people, and to save them trouble. He wanted to be thought kind and helpful, just as the doctor was. And soon everyone welcomed him when he

delivered the medicine, and offered him sweets and cakes, lemonade and milk.

But Twiddle wouldn't take anything. He was afraid the doctor would be cross.

For three weeks the little pixie stayed with Doctor Hey-Ho, and then one night the doctor spoke to him.

"Twiddle, you're cured," he said. "Of course, you know what was really the matter with you, don't you?"

Twiddle didn't answer. He just sat by the fire, and went very red.

"You were lazy and selfish," said the doctor. "You were a horrid, mean, unkind little pixie, spoilt by your kind old Aunt

Twinkle. Now you're a bright, cheerful hard-working fellow, and everyone tells me you are very kind and helpful. You're quite cured, so you can go home tomorrow."

Twiddle ran to Doctor Hey-Ho and hugged him.

"Thank you for curing me," he said. "I'll never get ill like that again, really I won't. And I have loved being here with you, so please let me come and stay with you sometimes, when you are very very busy, and want someone to do the housework."

"You shall!" said Doctor Hey-Ho. "I have loved having you, for you're not at all a bad little chap, really. You have made me very happy."

Wasn't Twiddle pleased when he heard that! He went to bed singing, and dreamed lovely dreams all night long.

Next day he packed his little bag, said goodbye to the doctor, and set off once more for the village of Kind-Heart. He whistled as he went along, and swung his bag as if it were as light as a feather.

39

"Why, here's Twiddle back again!" cried the villagers when they saw him coming. "Dear old Twiddle! Doesn't he look different! So happy and well and cheerful! Welcome back, Twiddle!"

The little pixie shook hands with everyone, and told them all how glad he was to see them. Then he ran to his own cottage, and knocked on the door with a glad heart. His aunt came to open it, and what a fuss she made of Twiddle. She hugged and kissed him, and almost cried over him, but he wouldn't let her.

"Aunt Twinkle," he said. "I was a very horrid pixie to you before I went away. I'm going to make up for it now, so please understand that in future I'm going to wait on you, and not you on me!"

He kept his word, and made Dame Twinkle very happy indeed. Everyone brought the pixie presents, and he accepted them with many thanks. But as soon as he had taken a pot of honey from someone, or some new scones, he would at once find out something he could do for them in return.

He was always doing odd jobs of weeding, sweeping, sawing wood or fetching water, and soon there was no one that was better-loved than Twiddle.

"Doctor Hey-Ho is wonderful!" they all said. "Why, he cured Twiddle of his dreadful illness in a few weeks, and look at him now! He's the merriest, nicest pixie that ever you could see!"

Doctor Hey-Ho smiled when he heard that. Nobody knew how he had cured Twiddle, and he never told anyone. Nor did the pixie, for he was ashamed to think he should ever have had to be cured.

Twice every year Twiddle goes to help Doctor Hey-Ho, and for two weeks he works harder than ever he worked before. But he loves it! So I really think he is cured for good and always – don't you?

The Bowl of
Bread and Milk

Someone had put a bowl of bread and milk out into the garden. Little Angelina Brown wouldn't eat her breakfast, so it had been taken away from her, and put outside.

The blackbird saw it first, and cocked his head on one side. "Tirrtoo!" he sang. "What a lovely feast!" and he flew down to have some.

Then the tiny mouse who lived under the toolshed smelled it, and popped his head out. "Squeak!" he said. "What a lovely feast!" and he ran over to the bowl.

Then who should come scuttling by but the hedgehog who lived in the ditch at the bottom of the garden. He suddenly saw the bread and milk and he stood still in delight. "Ooh!" he said. "What a lovely feast!" He ran over to the bowl, and there he met the blackbird and the mouse.

"Go away!" cried the blackbird, pecking the mouse with his strong, yellow beak. "This is my bread and milk!"

"You go away!" squeaked the mouse, angrily. "I'm sure I saw this first. It's mine, you greedy blackbird!"

"It's not yours or the blackbird's," said the hedgehog, putting his snout over the edge of the bowl. "It's mine, so go away, both of you. I am very hungry this morning, so I shall finish this all up."

Then the blackbird made an angry noise, and flew at him. He pecked him on the nose, and the hedgehog fell over on to the mouse, pricking him with his spines. The mouse squeaked in fright and nibbled one of the feathers in the blackbird's tail.

"Go away!" shouted the blackbird. "This is my bread and milk!"

"Go away!" cried the hedgehog. "This is my bread and milk!"

"Go away!" squeaked the mouse. "This is my bread and milk!"

But none of them would go away, and they chased each other all round the bowl, making a most tremendous noise.

Now not very far away, on top of the garden wall, was Whiskers, the big black cat. He was fast asleep in the warm sunshine, but soon the loud noise made by the blackbird, the mouse and the hedgehog woke him up with a start. He sat up and looked round.

Then he saw the bowl of bread and milk and the three quarrelsome creatures fighting for it. He got up and stretched himself. Then he jumped down from the wall and made his way slowly towards the bread and milk.

The blackbird suddenly saw him and gave a squawk of fright. He flew away into a nearby tree. Then the mouse saw him, and squeaked in terror. He ran away to his hole and hid himself there in safety. Then the hedgehog caught sight of the cat, too, and at once curled himself up into a spiky ball, and lay as still as if he were dead.

The cat took no notice of any of them. He went to the bowl and sniffed at it. Then he gave a purr of content and began to lap up the milk and eat the bread quickly, for he was very hungry. After that he sat down and carefully washed himself all over, not forgetting behind his ears, for he was a very clean cat. Then he went back to his place on the wall, lay down and fell fast asleep again.

The blackbird flew down to the empty bowl, and the mouse crept near. The hedgehog unrolled himself and put his snout over the edge.

"It's quite empty," he said, with a sigh.

"Quite," said the blackbird.

"All gone," said the little mouse, and a tear splashed on to his nose.

"How foolish we were to quarrel about it!" said the blackbird. "There was enough and to spare for all of us, if only we had been content to share it in peace. With our quarrelling we woke that horrid cat, and now there is no bread and milk left at all."

"We will be good to one another in future," said the hedgehog.

"Yes, let's," said the mouse.

"And as for that horrid cat," said the blackbird in a very loud voice, "he will be punished one day!"

The cat woke up, and heard what the blackbird said. He leaped down and sprang towards the three round the bowl – but no one was there!

The blackbird was at the top of a tree, the mouse was in his hole, and the hedgehog hurrying to his ditch.

"Silly things!" said the cat, and washed himself all over again, to show everyone that he didn't care what was said about him.

Mr Stamp-About
Loses His Temper

Mr Stamp-About didn't like the snow. For one thing it made him walk slowly, and he didn't like that, because he liked to stamp about in a hurry. And for another thing the small boys always lay in wait for him, and threw snowballs at his big hat.

The worst of it was that they could run much faster than old Stamp-About, and by the time he had got the snow out of his collar, and picked up his hat again, there was never anyone to be seen!

"Wait till I catch you! Just wait!" stormed Mr Stamp-About, stamping in the snow till he had made it quite flat and slippery. But, of course, nobody ever did wait to be caught by Mr Stamp-About.

"The little wretches never knock off

Mr Twiddle's hat," he said. "It's always mine! I'm always the one people play tricks on, and I don't like it. The very next time it happens I'll complain to Mr Plod the policeman. Yes, I will."

So he did. A well-aimed snowball not only knocked off his hat, but the snow spread itself all over his face, too, and he couldn't see anything for a minute or two. You can guess how he roared and stamped about! And off he went to find Mr Plod.

"I've been snowballed again!" he shouted at Mr Plod. "My hat's a wreck! I've icy snow water all down my neck! Why don't you catch the little pests who do this to me? What's a policeman for, I'd like to know?"

"Now, now, Mr Stamp-About," said Mr Plod. "No need to shout at me. I'm not the one who played tricks on you. And how can I catch anyone if I don't know who they are? You don't even know their names to tell me."

"How can I know them?" roared Stamp-About. "They hide till I come – and then I'm so blinded by snow I can't see them."

"If you could just *catch* one of them," said Mr Plod, and Mr Stamp-About almost blew him over with his scornful snort.

"Pooh! Catch one! They're as slippery as eels. Aha – if ever I do I'll tie him up properly, and bring him to you, Mr Plod. And I hope you'll put him in prison."

"Well, you bring him to me and I'll see," said Mr Plod. "Now, I've no more time to listen to you this morning, Mr Stamp-About, so don't begin all over again."

Mr Stamp-About wasn't used to being spoken to like this, and he went purple in the face. But he couldn't say another word because Mr Plod picked up the telephone and began to have a very important conversation with the Inspector. Mr Stamp-About really didn't dare to interrupt. So he went out, muttering angrily. If only he could catch somebody playing a trick on him!

Now, that evening Mr Stamp-About had to go and see his old friend, Mr Loud-Voice, who was ill with a cold, and was very upset because he had lost his voice. Mr Stamp-About stamped about his room, talking loudly, and poor Mr Loud-Voice was quite glad when at last he went.

It was when he was going home that things began to happen to Mr Stamp-About. He was walking along by Dame Old-One's house when suddenly something struck him.

It was snow! It struck Mr Stamp-About on the head, and quite knocked him over! He fell to the ground and the snow trickled down his neck in the horrible cold way it has.

Mr Stamp-About was looking for his hat when he was struck by something again – and once more he sank down under a mass of snow! He struggled up, and glared all round. Who was this, throwing enormous snowballs at him in the night? Who was it? If only he could see them!

Aha! What was that? A figure hiding over there, at the corner? There was

nobody else in sight. That was the wicked snowball-thrower! He thought Mr Stamp-About couldn't see him in the darkness, did he?

Mr Stamp-About didn't bother about his hat. Let it stay in the snow! He crept over the road, and then suddenly threw himself on the waiting figure, with a very fierce cry indeed. "Got you! Got you at last!"

Down went his victim into the snow, his face buried in it so that he could only gasp and splutter. He began to struggle. He was big and strong, which did not surprise Mr Stamp-About at all. Anyone able to throw such enormous snowballs must certainly be very strong!

But Stamp-About was bigger and stronger. He soon managed to tie up arms and ankles with his tie and his belt. Then, because the fellow was heavy, he dumped him back in the snow and tied up his mouth with his handkerchief so that he couldn't call for help.

"And now," said Mr Stamp-About to the struggling, trussed-up fellow, "I'm

off to the police station to get Mr Plod –
and you'll soon find yourself spending
the night in prison! Aha! I'll teach you to
go about throwing snowballs at a person
like me!"

Off he went. He soon arrived at the
police station and shouted for Mr Plod.
Mr Plod's assistant looked out of his
room.

"Mr Plod's out on his rounds," he said.
"Anything I can do?"

"I want you to come and arrest a fellow who's been lying in wait for me, and threw such enormous snowballs at me that I was completely buried under them," said Mr Stamp-About, fiercely.

"Oh, I'll have to wait until Mr Plod comes back," said the assistant. "Can't leave the police station with nobody in it, you know. Where's this fellow?"

"Tied up at the corner," said Stamp-About. "You come along and take him to prison."

"I tell you, we must wait till Mr Plod comes back," said the assistant. "Anyway, if the fellow is all tied up he can wait. Do him good."

So, very patient indeed, Mr Stamp-About sat down and waited for Mr Plod. And Mr Plod didn't come. "Must be on a case," said the assistant. "Burglary or something. Don't worry about the prisoner you've left out in the snow. I tell you it'll do him good to think about things a bit."

"I daresay – but I want to get home to bed," snapped Mr Stamp-About. "It's cold in here. I'm getting tired of waiting."

But still Mr Plod didn't come. And then at last, just as the police station clock was striking midnight, Mr Stamp-About heard voices.

"There's Mr Plod!" said the assistant, pleased. "But doesn't he sound angry. I wonder what's happened."

Mr Plod stalked into the police station, red with anger and shivering with cold. With him were two villagers, Old Man Wise and Father Wait-A-Bit.

"Sorry I'm so late," he said to his gaping assistant. "Some idiot leaped on me in the dark, got my face down in the snow and tied me up so that I couldn't shout or move! Wait till I get him. Just wait!"

"If I hadn't heard him muttering behind the hanky that was tied across his mouth he wouldn't have been found till morning," said Old Man Wise.

"We just managed to untie him before he fainted with the cold," said Father Wait-A-Bit. "What a shocking thing it is that anyone should dare to attack and tie up our own policeman. The fellow must be punished!"

"And sent to prison for five years," said Old Man Wise.

"No, twenty years!" raged Mr Plod, trying to get warm by the fire.

Now, Mr Stamp-About had been listening to all this in great surprise and horror. What – it was Mr Plod he had tied up – the policeman himself? Good gracious! What a truly terrible thing to have done!

Mr Stamp-About began to edge out of the room. The assistant saw him. "Oh, wait a minute – you wanted to ask . . ."

But Stamp-About no longer wanted to ask anyone anything. All he wanted was to get home to bed and hope that Mr Plod wouldn't hear anything about his waiting there all evening for him to arrest somebody that he, Stamp-About, had pounced on and tied up in the snow!

He went back home as quickly as he could. He suddenly remembered his hat. Where was it? Oh yes, he had left it buried in the snow by Dame Old-One's house! He had better go and get it.

He was fumbling in the snow there when suddenly he was struck down again. *Whoooosh!* Snow covered Stamp-About from head to foot! He sat down in a hurry, buried in snow.

What! Was there still someone about waiting to throw snowballs at him? No, it couldn't be. It must be – yes, it must be snow sliding off Dame Old-One's roof! It wasn't someone throwing enormous snowballs at him after all.

Whoooooooo. . . began the snow on the roof again, and Stamp-About just skipped

aside in time before another fall of snow crashed down. The snow everywhere was melting and here and there it was sliding off the steeper roofs, falling into gardens and on to pavements.

"I've been an idiot," said Mr Stamp-About, as he hurried home. "I thought a roof-fall was a snowball – I pounced on Mr Plod thinking he was the one who had thrown the snow at me – and goodness knows what he'll do to me tomorrow when he hears all I've done. Prison for twenty years, he said. Well, I shouldn't be surprised!"

Poor Mr Stamp-About. He didn't go to sleep all night – and now it's morning and he's waiting to hear the footsteps of the policeman come plod-plod-plodding down the street. Well, well – unpleasant things always happen when people stamp about and lose their tempers!

When Billy
Went to Granny's

Billy was very excited because he was to go to Granny's for the night! It was the first time he had stayed away from home. His mother packed his pyjamas in a bag, and also his toothbrush and sponge and hairbrush.

"There!" she said. "It is all ready for you, Billy. When Granny comes for you, pick up your bag and go with her. I am going to catch the bus now, but your sister Jane is upstairs, so goodbye, darling."

"Can I take one of my toys with me?" asked Billy. "Just one, Mummy?"

"Yes, just one," said his mother, looking round the bedroom to see which one. "Look, Billy, your new sailor doll looks very grand and smart. Take him to

Granny's. He will be pleased to go with you."

Billy ran down the stairs with his mother to see her catch the bus. The toys in his bedroom looked at one another, and the sailor doll got up and walked grandly across the floor.

"Did you hear what Billy's mother said?" said Sailor Doll. "Aha! I'm to go to stay for the night with Billy at his granny's! What do you think of that!"

"I wish I could go," said the old blue cat. "I have always slept with Billy each night and I would so like to go to his granny's with him."

"Pooh! You!" cried the sailor doll, scornfully. "A dirty, ragged old thing like you, with only one ear and a nibbled tail!"

"I can't help my tail," said the old blue cat. "That's where the puppy nibbled it once. And my ear I lost when I fell into a blackberry bush. And you'd be as dirty as I am too, if you were as old as me. Why, I am nearly as old as Billy."

"Well, Billy couldn't possibly take you away to stay with him," said Sailor Doll, looking down his bright pink nose at the cat. "His granny would throw you into the dustbin at once."

The old blue cat shivered and trembled. No toy likes to hear the word "dustbin". It is so dreadful to be thrown away. The sailor doll took a hairbrush belonging to the curly-haired doll and brushed his blue velvet suit carefully. He took off his sailor hat and banged it well. He polished up his shoes. My, he was smart, to be sure!

Presently Billy's grandmother came to fetch him and Billy ran to his bedroom

to get his bag. He looked round for the sailor doll.

"Come along, Sailor!" he said. "You are just as smart as I am! We shall enjoy ourselves at Granny's!"

He didn't even say goodbye to the other toys, though the old blue cat looked at him hard out of his black boot-button eyes. No – he was too excited to think of anyone but Sailor.

The old blue cat sat in the cupboard

and thought about Billy. He remembered how Billy had hugged him at night when he was very small. He remembered how once he had fallen out of Billy's cot, and Billy had cried till Mother put him back again. He remembered all the tea-parties that he had gone to, when Billy had put out the teacups and saucers. Oh, the old blue cat remembered heaps of things, and he missed Billy very much.

"I hope Sailor Doll will be nice to Billy tonight when he goes to bed," he thought. "Billy may feel a bit lonely, away from his mummy. He may want something to cuddle. Sailor Doll is not very cuddlesome or kind."

The sailor doll was having a marvellous time. He sat up in a chair at lunchtime and watched Billy eat. He went out in Granny's car with Billy in the afternoon, and saw a great many shops. He sat by Billy at teatime and Billy even gave him a bit of cake. The sailor doll felt very grand and very important.

"That is a fine sailor doll of yours," said Granny at teatime. "How well he behaves!"

"He is my newest toy," Billy said. "Uncle Dick bought him for me."

Sailor nearly fell off his chair with pride. My goodness gracious, what a lot he would have to tell the toys when he went back home!

When bedtime came the sailor doll watched Billy have a bath. He watched him get into his pyjamas and clean his teeth. He watched him brush his hair. He watched him say his prayers, and he watched him get in to bed. Granny kissed Billy goodnight, and put the doll into his cot.

"Goodnight, darling," she said. Then

she turned out the light. And it was just at that very minute that Billy felt a bit lonely. He wanted his mother there to tuck him up. But he was a big boy, so he didn't make a fuss. He just reached out his arm and felt for Sailor Doll.

"If I have something to cuddle I shall feel all right," thought Billy. "I shan't feel lonely then."

But the sailor doll didn't like being cuddled. It crushed his smart suit. It made him too hot. It was uncomfortable. He wriggled away, and wouldn't let Billy cuddle him.

And would you believe it, Billy began to cry! Yes, he really did! Granny heard him and came running in.

"What's the matter, darling?" she said. "Are you feeling a bit lonely?"

"Granny, I wish I had brought my old blue cat with me instead of Sailor Doll," said Billy. "He just won't be cuddled. My old blue cat cuddles up so warm and cosy. I wish I had him."

"I'll send Grandpa round home to get him," said Granny. "Don't worry. In ten

minutes you shall have the old blue cat!"

And sure enough, in ten minutes' time Grandpa came back with the old blue cat and gave him to Billy. And Billy cuddled him up, and the old blue cat snuggled as close as he could, and got warm and cosy and soft, and was as happy as could be! As for the sailor doll, he sat out on the chest-of-drawers all night by himself, and felt cold and lonesome. But it was his own fault, wasn't it?

Billy soon fell asleep, and the old blue cat slept too. He was so old that he snored a little bit, but he was very happy and comfortable, and so was Billy.

When Billy and Sailor Doll and the old blue cat got back to the nursery, what a lot of questions the toys there wanted to ask! And as soon as Billy had gone to play in the garden the sailor doll began to tell them all about his visit.

"And do you know," cried the sailor doll, "when bedtime came, Billy wanted the old blue cat – that dirty, nibbled creature! He's welcome to him, I'm sure – I didn't want to be cuddled and crushed. I'm sure he was ashamed of him, really – and he's so proud of me! You should have heard the things they said about me!"

"What have you got to say, old blue cat?" asked the teddy bear in his deep voice.

"Only this," said the old blue cat happily, "it is true that Billy is proud of Sailor Doll – but he doesn't love him. He isn't proud of me, I'm sure – but I know

70

he loves me very much. And it is better to be loved and cuddled, toys, than to be admired and put on the chest-of-drawers at night!"

"You are right, old blue cat!" said all the toys together. And dear me, didn't Sailor Doll feel small! Maybe he will learn to be nicer some day. What do you think?

The Knotty
Handkerchief

Once upon a time Too-Hot went to shell
peas in his garden. He took out a chair, a
basket of peas and a dish to put them in.
He sat down in the sunshine and began to
shell the peas.

It was a hot summer's day. It really
was very hot. Too-Hot puffed and panted,
and wished he had brought out a hat
to wear. He was too lazy to go in and
get one so he took out his big yellow
handkerchief and made it into a nice cap
by tying a knot in each of the four
corners. Then he slipped it on his head
and wore it like that. It kept the blazing
sun off his head.

When he had finished shelling the
peas he went indoors. He took off his
handkerchief cap and put it into his

pocket, quite forgetting to untie the knots. There it stayed till the next day.

When Too-Hot got up next morning he pulled his yellow handkerchief out of his pocket to put in a clean one – and then he discovered that it had a knot in each corner.

Now Too-Hot always tied a knot in his handkerchief when he wanted to remind himself to remember something. He used to tie a knot when he wanted to buy some more bacon for breakfast, and he always tied one when he wanted to remember to take his little dog for a

walk. So when he saw that his handkerchief had four knots in, he was most puzzled. It must have been something very important that made him tie four knots in, he thought.

He had forgotten that he had used his handkerchief for a sun-cap! He sat down and thought hard for five minutes.

"Now what made me tie so many knots?" he wondered. "Oh, dear, I wish I could remember! Is it somebody's birthday today? Or is somebody coming to tea with me? Or am I supposed to go and visit somebody? Whatever can it be? My dreadful memory! Oh, I wish I knew why I had tied all those knots in my handkerchief!"

Well, of course, Too-Hot couldn't remember why he had put those knots there, and it worried him dreadfully. He decided to go to Think-a-Lot the wise man and see if he could tell him the reason. So he took his purse and went.

Think-a-Lot looked at the yellow handkerchief with all the knots in, and frowned. He put it into a saucepan of

purple milk and boiled it for five minutes. Then he took out the handkerchief, which was now spotted with purple, and squeezed it dry. He opened it and looked closely at it. Across it was written one word.

"Here's the reason that you knotted your handkerchief," he said. "It's written across it for you to read."

Too-Hot looked closely at it. "It says 'sunshine'!" he said. "Sunshine! Now whatever does that mean? Why should

I have knotted my handkerchief to remember sunshine? Dear, dear, dear, it's a greater puzzle than ever!"

He paid the wise man a silver sixpence, and went away, frowning hard. Sunshine? What did it mean? Was he to put something out in the sun to dry? Was that what he had wanted to remind himself to do?

Too-Hot couldn't think of anything at all. So he decided to go up the Tall Hill to Breezy Cottage, where Know-It-All the brownie lived. Know-It-All was very clever, and had such a good memory that he could often remember what other people forgot.

So up the Tall Hill went Too-Hot, carrying his knotty yellow handkerchief. Know-It-All was sitting outside his door, knitting a scarf of field-mist, very fine and delicate. It was wonderful to watch him. He greeted Too-Hot with a smile and asked him what he wanted.

"I want to know if you can tell me why I put four knots in this handkerchief," said Too-Hot. "I always tie knots in my

76

handkerchief when I want to remember anything important, but this time I can't remember why I tied the knots! Could you tell me, do you think?"

Know-It-All took the handkerchief and felt all the knots with a very wise look on his face. Then he took it indoors and, to Too-Hot's surprise and dismay, threw the handkerchief on to the fire. But it didn't burn. No, it simply lay there,

turning blue, then green, then red, and suddenly it jumped right out of the fire and landed at Know-It-All's feet.

The brownie picked it up and rubbed it between his hands. All the knots had turned green, so the handkerchief looked a bit peculiar now. It was yellow with purple spots and green knots!

"Here you are," said Know-It-All, handing it to Too-Hot. "You'll find the reason for your knots written across it."

Too-Hot took it and looked at it. The first word, "sunshine", had gone and in its place was written "too hot".

"Too hot!" said Too-Hot, astonished. "Now what does that mean? That's my name – why should that be written across the handkerchief?"

"Well, I expect you wanted to remind yourself not to let something get too hot," said Know-It-All. "Didn't you, now?"

"No, I don't think so," said Too-Hot, puzzled. "Now, let me see – what gets too hot? I don't like to let my kitchen stove get too hot – but that hasn't a fire in this summer weather. So I can't have wanted to remind myself of that. It's very difficult to find out the meaning of these four knots, isn't it, Know-It-All?"

"It seems to be," said Know-It-All, taking up his knitting again. "That will be a silver sixpence, please, Too-Hot."

Too-Hot paid his silver sixpence and went off again, still worried and puzzled. He looked in his purse. He had one silver sixpence left. He would go to Dame Squeeze and see if she could tell him why he had tied four knots in his handkerchief. Then he couldn't go to anybody else because he would have spent all his money.

Dame Squeeze lived in the middle of Ho-Ho Wood. Too-Hot made his way there and knocked at her front door. Dame Squeeze opened it and told Too-Hot to come inside.

"What do you want?" she asked. "I'm very busy with a new spell, so don't stop long."

Too-Hot told her what he wanted.

"That's easy," said Dame Squeeze. "Give me the handkerchief."

She took it and undid each of the four knots. She put a pat of butter in one corner and knotted it up again. She put a yellow feather in another corner and knotted that up. She put a dab of honey in the third corner and a fish-tail in the last one. When they were all knotted up once more she stood on the handkerchief and said a few magic words.

Then she picked it up and opened it out. The handkerchief was in a terrible mess now – greasy with the butter, sticky with the honey and smelly with the fish-tail.

"It's got 'cap' written across it," said

80

Dame Squeeze, showing the handkerchief to Too-Hot. "You must have tied
those knots because of a cap of some
sort."

"But I'm sure I didn't want to
remember anything about a cap," said

81

Too-Hot, more puzzled than ever. "Oh dear, it's a mystery! I'm afraid I shall never know why I knotted those four knots. Thank you, Dame Squeeze. You haven't really helped me at all, but here is a silver sixpence."

Too-Hot went home sadly, wishing he hadn't spent all his money.

"I'll have some fried potatoes for my lunch," he said to himself. "I can't buy anything because I haven't any money."

He took a dish of potatoes and went into the garden to peel them. He sat down in the sunshine and began. The sun was very hot on his head and he wished he had brought out a hat.

"I'll make myself a handkerchief cap," he thought. "I'll put a knot in each corner and then it will make a nice sun-cap for me – just like I did yesterday!"

He took out his handkerchief and stared at it. It was yellow with purple spots and green knots in the corner. It was greasy and sticky and smelled of fish.

"Oh my, oh my, oh my, what a silly

stupid I've been!" poor Too-Hot cried suddenly! "I didn't put those knots in to remember anything! I just put them in to make myself a sun-cap when I was shelling peas in the sunshine yesterday! That's why the handkerchief had 'sunshine' and 'too hot' and 'cap' written across it – and I never guessed. Oh, what a foolish person I am! And to think I've spent all my money too. Oh, it's enough to make anyone cry his eyes out!"

And Too-Hot began crying and weeping as if his heart would break, but whether he really cried his eyes right out I don't know. I shouldn't be surprised if he did, for he was too foolish for anything, wasn't he?

The Two
Rough Children

There were once two rough children. Some children have nice manners, and some haven't. Well, Katie and Sam hadn't! How the other children hated them!

Sam was always coming up to them and slapping them so hard on the back that they nearly fell over. And Katie loved to pinch people and pull their hair. Sometimes Sam tickled another boy or girl – and how his hard fingers did hurt! And often Katie slapped people so hard that it made them blink tears away from their eyes.

Now you might think that the other children would soon slap back, and pinch and punch too – but they didn't, because Sam and Katie were both so big for their age. The other children were half afraid of them. So they did their best to keep out of their way, but that wasn't much good, you may be sure.

Now one day, to Sam's great surprise and Katie's too, they had an invitation to a party. The card didn't come through the post, but was left on the seat in their garden, which was rather strange. Katie opened the blue envelope and this is what she read:

The Knockabout Goblins are giving a party on Tuesday night at twelve o'clock in the buttercup field. Please come.

Well! Sam and Katie stared at one another in delight and surprise. A fairy party! With goblins! Perhaps there would be a dance – and they might even see the Fairy King and Queen! Oooh, what a treat!

"I expect the other children have been asked too," said Sam. But to their great surprise they found that no other child had had an invitation. They were the only ones.

That made the two children feel very proud indeed. "We are the only ones asked!" said Katie, and she felt so pleased that she slapped the girl standing near her.

"Aren't you sorry you're left out?" said Sam, and he punched Alan hard for nothing at all. Those two children simply could not keep their big hands to themselves.

Well, the night came. Sam and Katie went to bed as usual – but they didn't go to sleep, as you can imagine! When half-past eleven came, Katie put on her best party frock with red ribbons, and Sam put on his checked shirt and shorts. Then they crept out of the house and ran to the buttercup field.

As soon as they got near they could hear the sounds of a party. Oh, what fun! They heard a drum going *Boom-boom, boom*, and fiddles squeaking high, *Eee-eee-eee*! and trumpets sounding loud, *Toot-ti-toot, toot-ti-toot*!

They got to the stile – and what a sight they saw! There were about a hundred goblins in the buttercup field, all nearly as big as the children, and all racing about like mad, and shouting and jumping. Suddenly they saw the two children and they ran to the stile.

"Here are Sam and Katie! Come on, children! We did hope you would come. We were not allowed to ask any one else but you."

The goblins pulled the children into the field. "Dance with me!" said a fat goblin to Katie, and he held her tightly. Sam was taken round and round by three goblins, in a dance he didn't know at all.

It was a dreadful dance. The thing to

do was to bump into everyone else at top
speed, and then shout with laughter.
Then other goblins bumped into you and
tried to make you fall on the ground.
Katie didn't like it. As for poor Sam, he
had a very rough time of it with his three
goblins, for they swung him round so
fast that he got giddy. They bumped him

into about fifty others, and then at last they fell to the ground, with Sam underneath.

The music stopped. Katie looked at her pretty party frock. It was torn and dirty already. What would her mother say? A goblin came up and screeched loudly in her ear: "EEEEEEEEEE! I'm an engine going through a tunnel. EEEEEEEEE!"

This was a thing that Sam and Katie often did to scare other children – and now Katie was so scared herself that she ran away. But the goblin put out his hand and caught hold of her by her red ribbons – and they came off and tore a hole in her frock. Instead of saying he was sorry, the goblin grinned and tied the ribbons round his own head.

"Don't do that!" cried Katie angrily. But the goblin only danced round her and laughed.

Then someone began to shout, "A ring, a ring – make a ring! We're going to play the slapping game!"

So a large ring was made, and Sam

and Katie were pushed inside it. "How do we play this game?" asked Sam. "I don't know it."

"Oh, you run round the ring and try to get in somewhere," said the goblin. "And as you pass we can slap you. It's a fine game!"

Well, it may have been a fine game for the goblins, but it wasn't at all nice for Sam and Katie. As they ran round the ring, trying their hardest to squeeze into it, the goblins unlinked their hard, horny hands and slapped the children.

Slap! Smack! SLAP! Thwack! Slippity-slap!

Katie began to cry. The slaps hurt. "Don't do that!" she sobbed. "Don't do that!"

Sam got such a hard slap that he lost his temper. He turned on the goblin who had slapped him.

"If you do that again you'll be sorry!" he said. The goblin did it again – *SLAP*! Sam kicked him – and at once a shout went up.

"The kicking game! The kicking game!" Before the children knew what was happening the goblins had made two long lines, with the children in the middle.

"Go on, Sam – go on, Katie!" cried the top goblin. "Run down the lines as fast as you can. This is the kicking game."

By now the two children wanted to get back home as quickly as they could, so they ran down between the two lines at top speed – and do you know, as they went those horrible little Knockabout Goblins tried to kick them. Poor Sam and Katie! How bruised and sore they felt!

"I hate this, Katie," said Sam. "Whatever will they do next?"

The next game was something to do with pinching and pulling, and Katie turned quite pale. She was sure that she would be pinched and pulled about, and the goblins were so strong that it really wasn't much good trying to pinch and pull back. But just as the game was about to begin, there came a great silence, and suddenly every goblin fell down on one knee.

The children looked up. A fairy with a beautiful face and long silver wings trailing behind her had just flown down.

"The Princess! The Princess Peronel!" cried everyone.

"Good evening, goblins," said the princess in a voice like the twittering of a swallow. "I hope your party is a good one?"

"Fine, fine!" cried the goblins.

"And I hope your two guests are enjoying it too," said Peronel, looking

kindly at Sam and Katie. The children were kneeling, like the goblins, for they felt it must be the right thing to do.

Katie burst into tears. "It's a hateful, horrid, nasty party!" she sobbed. "My dress is spoilt and torn. I have been smacked and slapped and kicked, and so has Sam. If I'd known it was to be such a rough party I wouldn't have come."

Princess Peronel looked surprised. "But you love being rough," she said. "I've often watched you in the playground at school, slapping and pushing and pinching and poking. I always let the Knockabout Goblins ask two children to their party, and I thought, as you loved rough things, you would enjoy the party."

Sam and Katie went red. They didn't know what to say.

"You do like being rough, don't you?" said Peronel, still looking puzzled.

"Yes," said Katie, wiping her eyes. "I suppose we do – but we don't like it when people are rough to us!"

"Oh, but that's not fair!" said Peronel, suddenly looking stern. "Not fair at all.

Do the others like it when you are rough to them?"

"No," said Sam. "I see what you mean, Princess. We've been doing what people hate – and we hate it too, when it's done to us. Please let us go home. We've learned our lesson."

"Well, you may go," said Peronel. "But be careful not to come near the buttercup field again if you act roughly – because the Knockabout Goblins will love to play with you again, you know."

The children got up from their knees and ran home at once, not even looking behind to see what the goblins were doing. And do you suppose they pinch and punch and slap and smack now? My goodness, no! They don't want to play with the Knockabout Goblins again, you may be sure.

Sandy Rabbit's Party

Soon Sandy Rabbit would be two years old, and he meant to have a party. He felt most excited and rubbed his paws together in delight.

"My birthday is at the end of October!" he said. "It is now the beginning. I shall send out all my invitations at once!"

So he sat down and wrote six cards in his very best handwriting, and then sent them off. They went to Slinky the snake, Flitter the bat, Derry the dormouse, Prickles the hedgehog, Crawler the toad, and Big-One the badger.

Everyone accepted. Parties did not come very often, and nobody meant to miss this one. Sandy Rabbit was known to be generous, and all the guests felt sure that they would have a fine feast.

"There will be a few frogs for me!" thought Slinky the snake.

"There are sure to be fat flies for me!" squeaked Flitter the bat.

"There will be hazel nuts for me and a few acorns," said Derry the dormouse.

"Beetles and grubs for me!" decided Prickles the hedgehog.

"A dozen bluebottle flies for me!" croaked Crawler the toad.

"I should enjoy a few mice and lizards," grunted Big-One the badger.

Sandy Rabbit knew perfectly well what all his guests liked best, and all that month he set about getting his birthday feast ready. Goodness! What a larderful

he had! He hired a large table and bought a new blue-checked tablecloth. He knitted himself a new yellow scarf, and had his whiskers nicely trimmed. He meant to look his best, and to give the finest party that had ever been heard of!

Towards the end of the month there came a very hard frost, when the earth was frozen and the wind was bitter. Sandy Rabbit didn't care! He grew a thicker coat and ran about to keep himself warm. The east wind blew hard, and all the trees grew bare and cold. The swallows all disappeared and the robin fluffed out his feathers and thought it was time to go and tap at the window of the little girl he knew. He wanted some crumbs.

Sandy Rabbit was very happy. His birthday was coming near, and his lovely, lovely party! When the day came at last it was bitterly cold and Sandy Rabbit put up his big table in the shelter of the hedgerow. He spread it with all his goodies, put on his new scarf, and then looked out eagerly for his guests.

But alas! Slinky the snake didn't come. Flitter the bat was nowhere to be seen, Derry the dormouse was not to be found. Prickles the hedgehog didn't arrive. Crawler the toad was not there – and as for Big-One the badger, no one had seen him for days.

Sandy Rabbit sat and cried by himself. "Nobody loves me!" he sobbed. "I expect they've all gone to someone else's party. Oh, how I wish I knew what had happened!"

Well, I know what had happened, and what all the guests were doing. Do you? If you do, write a note to Sandy Rabbit and tell him. He will be so pleased!

The Bed That
Ran Away

Once upon a time there was a small girl called Anna and a little boy called Guy. Guy was a wide-awake little fellow. But Anna – dear me, what a sleepyhead she was!

She would not wake up in the morning! She was always yawning, all the day long, and she was always ready to go to bed at night.

Her mother used to get very tired of trying to wake her up each morning. She would go into Anna's room and say:

"Anna. Wake up! Time to get up!"

No answer from Anna.

"ANNA! WAKE UP! You'll be late for school!"

"M-mm-m-mm," Anna would mumble, half asleep. Then her mother would pull all the clothes from her and cry "You lazy little girl! Get up, I say!"

Then she would go from the room, and that lazy little Anna would pull up the clothes again and go to sleep once more! So she hardly ever had time for a proper breakfast, and was always late for school.

One day her mother was so cross that she said she couldn't be bothered to wake up Anna any more.

"You can wake her up, Guy," she said. "Do what you like – squeeze a cold sponge over her head – take off the

blankets and put them on the other side of the room – but wake her up."

So Guy said he would – but dear me, it was difficult, because Anna could sleep even though cold water was pouring over her face, and when she found that her bedclothes were on the other side of the room, why, she just went to sleep again without them, curling up her toes inside her nightdress for warmth. She was a sleepyhead!

Now one of Guy's schoolfellows had a grandmother who was supposed to be a very wise woman. She often went out in the early mornings and picked strange herbs and leaves to make potions. She was a kindly old woman, always ready to help anyone, and Guy wondered if she would be able to tell him how to cure Anna of her sleepiness.

So one evening he went to call on her. She lived in a little cottage on the edge of the wood. The old dame opened the door herself and smiled at Guy.

"Hello, young man, and what can I do for you?" she asked.

Guy told her his trouble and she listened with a twinkle in her eye.

"A sleepyheaded sister," she said, when he had finished. "Well, we must certainly cure her, Guy, or she won't be a bit of use in the world."

"Can you cure her?" Guy asked eagerly.

"I'm not quite sure," said the old woman. She went to a drawer and opened it. In it were the strangest things Guy had ever seen – peacocks' feathers, sparkling powders, small dolls like pixies, shining butterflies' wings neatly piled together and tiny bottles of bright-coloured liquids.

The old dame took up a small yellow box and opened it. Inside were a number of very tiny shining stars, glittering brightly.

The old woman shook three out into her hand. "Now these," she said, "are supposed to be a sure cure for a sleepyhead. Put one under the pillow of a sleepy person and it is said he will be cured by the next day. If not put a second under his pillow the next night and a third the following night. After that he will wake up early each morning and never be a sleepyhead again. But these little stars are very old and may have lost their power, so don't trust too much to them, Guy. They may be no use at all. But you can try them if you like."

"Oh thank you!" cried Guy. He took an empty matchbox from his pocket and slipped the three curious stars inside it. They shone strangely and seemed full of magic.

"What do they do to make the sleepyhead wake up?"

"Oh, it is said that the bed makes a

curious creaking noise which frightens
the person in bed so much that he wakes
up at once!" said the old dame. "You
must watch and see what happens, Guy."

Guy thanked the old lady and said
goodbye, and ran home. What a secret he
had! He took out the little stars and
looked at them. Would they really be
powerful enough to cure such a sleepy
person as Anna? Surely a little creaking
and groaning wouldn't wake her up.

"I think I shall put all three stars
under her pillow," decided the little boy.
"Then perhaps the bed will make such a
loud noise that it will waken even Anna!"

So that night when Anna was fast

asleep in bed Guy stole up to her and slipped all three of the little shining stars under her pillow. Then off he went to his own bed, and left his door open so that he could hear when Anna's bed began to creak and groan.

At five o'clock in the morning, when the sun was just rising and all the world was golden, Guy woke up. Whatever was that noise? He sat up in bed and remembered. Ah, it was Anna's bed. How angry she would be to be wakened up at five o'clock!

He slipped out of his bed and ran to Anna's room. The little girl was lying fast asleep as usual – but the bed was behaving very strangely.

It groaned deeply. It creaked heavily. It tossed the mattress up and down as if it were trying to shake Anna out of bed. But she didn't move!

Guy stood and watched. It was a very strange thing to see. Then he saw something even stranger!

The bed lifted up one foot and pawed the floor with it like a horse! Guy didn't

like that much. It seemed far too weird!
Whatever would it do next?

It lifted up another foot and knocked
on the floor with that too – and then, oh
my goodness me, it began to move! Yes, it
really did! It walked towards the door,
creaking and groaning for all it was
worth, putting out first one foot and then

another, just as if it were a four legged animal!

Guy tried to push the bed back into its place but it tapped him smartly on the toe and made him jump. It pushed him away and squeezed itself through the door and then it jolted itself down the stairs! It made such a noise at the time, creaking like a dozen doors and grumbling to itself like a live thing. Guy didn't know what to do!

"Anna, Anna, wake up!" he cried. "Your bed is walking away with you!"

"Mm-m-mm-m-mm," said Anna, in her sleep.

"Anna! Get up!" shouted Guy, trying to roll the little girl out of bed. But she only curled herself up all the more tightly and slept soundly. It was quite impossible to wake her.

Guy was just going to run and waken his parents when he saw that the bed was beginning to run! It had got down the stairs and somehow or other the front door had opened and now the bed was out in the street, running along.

There was no time to get help! By the time he had wakened his mother the bed would be out of sight and nobody would know where Anna had gone! He must keep close to the bed, whatever happened. If only he could wake Anna.

The bed jogged on happily, creaking as it went. Guy ran after it, still in his pyjamas for he had had no time to dress. It ran faster. Guy ran fast too. The bed made for a little lane and rushed down it, almost galloping, so that Anna was jolted

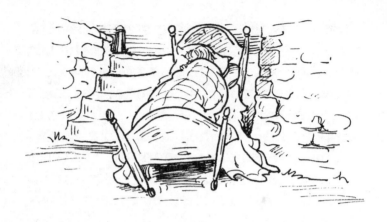

up and down, but still she didn't wake. Guy tore after the bed. It turned a corner and Guy ran to the corner too – but when he got there, the bed was gone.

"It's gone!" said Guy in horror. "Where is it?"

There was no bed to be seen. It had vanished into thin air. Not a creak, not a groan was to be heard. Poor Guy! Tears came into his eyes but he wiped them away. Crying wouldn't help Anna. No, he must go straight to the old woman who had given him those little shining stars and see if she could tell him where the bed had gone.

So off he went and the old dame was

most surprised to have such an early visitor. When she heard what had happened she sat down in amazement.

"You shouldn't have put all three stars under the pillow," she said at last. "Of course that would give the bed the power to run right away. One star just makes it want to go, and it creaks and groans because it can't – but three stars! Well, of course it would disappear!"

"But Anna didn't wake up," said Guy, in despair.

"She must be a sleepyhead!" said the old dame. "Well, well, we must see what we can do. The bed has gone to the Land of Nod, you know. Perhaps if we go there we can manage to rescue Anna."

"Oh, will you go with me?" asked Guy.

"Of course!" said the old dame. "Come and sit on my knee in my big armchair and it will take us to the Land of Nod, where we can look for poor Anna."

She sat down and Guy climbed up on to her knee. She began to tell him a story. It was a sleepy story and Guy, who was tired, gradually felt his head beginning to

nod. He would soon be asleep. The chair
began to rock, for it was a rocking chair.
It rocked and rocked, and at last it rocked
so hard that Guy opened his eyes in
surprise.

And do you know, it wasn't a chair
after all! It was a boat, rocking on a deep
blue sea. He was sitting on a soft cushion
and the old dame was sitting opposite to
him, smiling broadly.

"Well, here we are on the way to the Land of Nod," she said. "We shan't be long in this boat."

The sea stretched for ever around them – or so it seemed. No land was in sight anywhere. Fish gleamed in the depths of the blue like stars. Guy wished he could catch some.

"We're nearly there," said the old woman.

"Where?" asked Guy, in surprise. He could see nothing at all but sea.

And then, to his enormous surprise, a curious, cloudy land seemed to rise out of the blue sea just by him. It grew bigger and bigger, its towers shot up to the clouds, its palaces glimmered in the pale sunshine.

"That's the Land of Nod," whispered the old woman. "You mustn't make a noise here, in case you wake the sleepers."

"Who are they?" asked Guy.

"Oh, I expect Anna is one of them by now!" said the old dame, with a laugh.

The boat came softly to shore. The old

dame got out and helped Guy to the sand. There was no wind, not a sound of any sort to be heard.

"It's just like a dream," said Guy, in a whisper.

"Well, you can only come here in a dream, you know," said the old woman. "Now we must see if we can find Anna."

Nobody was in the blue misty streets. Guy's slippers seemed to make such a noise in that silent land.

Suddenly a white rabbit appeared, his long ears twitching forwards. When he saw Guy and the old woman he ran silently towards them.

"Take off your shoes, boy," he hissed. "Don't you know that if you wake anyone in the Land of Nod a nightmare will gallop up and carry you away and you'll never be seen again?"

"Ooh!" said Guy, in fright, taking off his slippers at once. He didn't want to be galloped off on the back of a nightmare!

The rabbit disappeared. The old woman pointed silently to a big palace not far off.

"That's where the sleepers are," she whispered. "Come on!"

They made their way to the palace. Its many pinnacles shone silvery in the early morning light. There was a great flight of steps up to a wide glass door.

The little boy and the old woman went softly up – and just as they reached the top a sound came to their ears! It came from behind them. They turned to look.

And whatever do you think they saw? Why, Anna's bed coming slowly up the steps! Yes, they had got to the Land of Nod first!

The bed, creaking softly, and groaning under its breath, came up the steps one foot after another – and Anna still lay there fast asleep! Would you believe it?

The bed pushed open the shining glass door and went inside. The other two followed. What a strange sight met their eyes in the palace! There was a long hall and on either side were beds – some big, some small, but all with sleepers in, curled up in slumber. Anna's bed wandered down the hall, as if it were looking for a place. There was none for it, so it went through another door and into a smaller room. Beds were here too, but still there was no room. Into yet another room went the bed, groaning to itself as if it were very tired.

In this third room there was a space big enough for one more bed. Anna's bed walked carefully backwards into it and then, with a soft creak of delight, stood perfectly still. It had found its place in the Land of Nod!

"How can we wake her?" asked Guy, in a whisper.

"You can't," said the old woman. "Nobody does anything but sleep here. We shall have to do the only thing we can – make the bed take her back home again."

"But how can we do that?" asked Guy, in surprise.

"If you can manage to take away the three little stars you put under Anna's pillow, I think the bed will have to go back," said the old dame. " It hasn't got rooted here yet, as all the others have. It has only just come. But I'm afraid it will be very angry."

Guy slipped down the side of the bed. He put his hand under Anna's pillow and felt about for the three little stars. It really seemed as if they didn't want to be taken away for they ran about under the pillow like live things, and pricked Guy's hand whenever they could. But at last he got hold of them, slipped them into his matchbox and gave them to the old woman.

"Now we'll see what happens," said the old dame. "Stand back a little."

As soon as the bed knew that the little magic stars were gone, it began to make a terrible noise, for it knew it would have to go back to where it came from. It began to creak as loudly as twenty wardrobes, and groan so deeply that even Guy jumped. Then it moved! First one foot and then the other, but what a noise it made! It knocked here, it stamped there, it even seemed to dance with rage. Anna was shaken up and down but she didn't wake up! The bed moved out of its corner and went down the room. It ran out of the door, stamping and creaking like a mad thing.

Then, suddenly, the palace was full of strange horses with gleaming eyes and long tails. The nightmares had come! They stamped their hoofs, and raced

about in anger. Guy felt frightened of them. He began to climb up on to a bed where a sleeper lay, lost in slumber – but the old woman pulled him off at once.

"You'll never go back home if you get into one of these beds!" she said. "The only thing you can do is to catch a nightmare and ride it. It will take you home all right, though I warn you it will not be a pleasant ride."

Guy did as he was told. He ran to one of the prancing coal-black nightmares and clambered on to its back. It threw up its head, made a whinnying noise and then galloped off at top speed. Guy clung on for all he was worth.

It was not a nice ride, as the old woman had said. The horse seemed to delight in giving poor Guy as many frights as it could. It galloped into a moonlit land and came to a high cliff. Far down below was the gleaming sea. The nightmare, instead of stopping at the edge of the cliff, jumped right over it!

Guy gave a gasp. Whatever would happen? Would they fall into the sea?

But no! The horse stretched out its wings in midair and flapped safely back to the cliff-edge, with Guy clinging tightly to its neck. It hrrumphed in delight when it saw how frightened Guy was.

Off it galloped again, and this time Guy saw a great wall in front of them. Surely the nightmare was not going to try and jump that! It would never get over the top.

But the horse gave a spring and up it went, with Guy wondering whatever would be on the other side. Over the top of the wall they went, and then Guy saw a swiftly-flowing river on the far side of the wall. *Splash!* Into it they went, and the horse began to swim. Two or three times waves splashed over Guy's shoulders and he swallowed some water.

The nightmare scrambled out the other side and galloped off again with Guy almost tumbling off. It went so fast that the little boy's hair streamed out in the wind. Faster and faster – faster and faster and faster! Guy clung on tightly. Goodness, surely the horse couldn't go much faster! Suddenly the animal put its hoof into a rabbit-hole and over it went. Guy shot up into the air and came down again with a bump.

He gasped and opened his eyes.

And would you believe it, he was at home! By him was his bed, and he was on the floor.

"Well, anyone would think I had tumbled out of bed," he thought, getting up. "Anyway, I'm safely back from the Land of Nod – but what about Anna?"

He ran to his sister's room – and was just in time to see the bed squeezing itself in at the door again, creaking and groaning. Anna was fast asleep, of course. The bed went to its place and stood perfectly still and silent. A clock downstairs struck seven.

His mother came out of her room.

"Hello, Guy," she said. "Do try to get Anna down in time for breakfast today."

Guy woke Anna up by pulling her out of bed and making her go bump on the floor. Then he sat down by her and told her all the extraordinary adventures of that morning, and how she had been to the Land of Nod and back.

"Oh!" said Anna, turning pale. "Do you know, I dreamed it, too! I knew everything that happened, but I couldn't wake up. Oh, Guy, just suppose I'd stayed there!"

"Well, if I were you I'd get up each morning as soon as you're called," said Guy, "just in case that bed of yours starts off again!"

"Oh, I will!" said Anna, and dressed in a hurry, anxious to get away from her peculiar bed. How surprised her mother was to see her down to breakfast ten minutes early!

The next morning, while Anna was still asleep, the bed creaked a little. My goodness, you should have seen Anna! She sat up in bed at once, leaped out and dressed as quickly as she could – and that bed has only got to give the smallest creak each day for Anna to be up and dressing in two shakes of a duck's tail!

"I'm not going to be taken off to the Land of Nod again!" she says – and I'm not surprised, are you?

Mother Dimity's
Best Dress

"Good gracious!" said Mother Dimity. "It's two o'clock, and that dressmaker hasn't sent me my best dress yet! The party begins at four. Whatever shall I do? Come here, Poppo, you must go and fetch my dress for me."

"Oh bother!" said Poppo, who was reading a most exciting book.

"Now don't say that!" said his mother, crossly. "Just run to Miss Snip's at once. Say you have come for my dress and she really must give it to you. You are not to stop on the way there or on the way back, for I really must have that dress at once."

"Can't I stop at the ginger-pop shop and have a drink?" asked Poppo. "It's a long, dusty road to Miss Snip's, Ma."

"You'll just not stop anywhere for anything!" cried his mother, pushing him out of the door. "Haven't I told you I must have my dress at once? If you waste any more time I'll not take you to the party with me, so there!"

Poppo ran off, grumbling. He went to Miss Snip's and found that she had just finished the dress, and was packing it up in a paper parcel.

"Here you are," she said. "Now run home quickly, Poppo, and don't keep your mother waiting."

Poppo turned homewards. The sun shone warmly and the road was dusty. Poppo got thirstier and thirstier. By the time he reached Dame Quickly's ginger-pop shop he felt that if he didn't have a drink, he would never get home.

"I'll just pop into the shop, have a glass of ginger beer, and pop out again," he thought. "Ma will never know. I'll be as quick as quick!"

So he popped in, put his penny down and asked for a drink. He placed his parcel on a chair, then took the glass

in his hands. Oh, what a lovely drink!
Poppo felt it running down his hot throat,
and wished that a glass of ginger beer
lasted as long as an hour.

"Thank you!" he said to Dame Quickly.
"Well, I musn't stay any longer. Goodbye,
everybody!"

Sandy Rabbit, Twinkles the Gnome,
Mixie Mole, and Dame Quickly waved
goodbye. Poppo ran out of the shop, the
parcel under his arm, and set off home. It
wasn't long before he got there, and gave
his mother the parcel.

"Good boy!" she said. "You haven't been long! Now I've just got nice time to go upstairs and change into my new dress. You wash yourself, Poppo, and brush your hair, then you'll be ready too."

She bustled upstairs with the parcel. She put it on the bed and cut the string. Then she undid the paper. When she saw what was in the parcel, she stared and stared and stared. Then she cried out in horror.

"Poppo! Poppo!" she cried. "There's nothing but a great big cabbage in this parcel! Where's my dress? What have you done with it? Oh dear, oh dear, whatever has happened?"

"Good gracious, Ma!" said Poppo, running upstairs and gazing in surprise at the very large cabbage on the bed. "What's happened to the dress? Why, I saw Miss Snip put it into the parcel!"

Mother Dimity began to sob and cry.

"Now I can't go to the party! Oh, what a piece of bad luck! Poppo, you just take this parcel straight back to Miss Snip,

and show her what was in it. Someone
must have put a spell on it!"

Poppo wrapped up the cabbage and
set off once again. Mother Dimity washed
her face, crying big tears into the basin
all the time for she was so disappointed.
Suddenly she heard a knock at the door
and she ran down to open it. On the step
stood old Dame Quickly of the ginger-
pop shop. Under her arm she held a
parcel.

"Good afternoon, ma'am," she said.

"This parcel was left in my shop this afternoon by your boy, Poppo. He took another one by mistake, which had a fine cabbage in that Mixie Mole had brought as a present to me. I thought you might be needing the dress, so I brought it along."

"Oh, thank you, thank you!" cried Mother Dimity, gladly. "But what was Poppo doing in your shop? I told him he wasn't to stop for a minute on his errand."

"He is a naughty boy, then," said Dame Quickly. "He came for a ginger beer, ma'am."

"Oho!" said Mother Dimity, as she shut the door and ran upstairs with the parcel. "Well, Poppo has had his punishment! He'll have gone all the way to Miss Snip's for nothing, and when he gets home he'll find I've gone to the party without him."

Poor Poppo! When he got to Miss Snip's she was quite cross with him for suggesting that the lovely dress she had made had had a spell put on it! So he went sadly home again.

On the way he passed the ginger-pop shop, and old Dame Quickly saw him.

"Hi, Poppo!" she called. "Come here! You've got my cabbage with you!"

"Your cabbage?" said Poppo in astonishment.

"Yes," said Dame Quickly. "You left your parcel here in mistake, and took mine. So I've taken your mother's dress to her. Now you can leave that cabbage here."

"Does my ma know I came here for a drink, after she'd told me not to?" asked Poppo.

"She does," said Dame Quickly. "You're

a very naughty boy, that's what you are! And you won't go to the party now, and it serves you right!"

Poppo ran home. When he got there he found the house empty. His mother had gone to the party without him. He was dreadfully upset.

"It's my own stupid fault!" he said. "If I hadn't been disobedient it wouldn't have happened. I must just make the best of it."

It was a lovely party, and halfway through it Mother Dimity felt very sorry for Poppo. So she asked if she might take a cream bun home to him, and a chocolate cake. He was pleased!

"Thank you, Ma," he said. "I'll be a better boy next time, really I will!"

Sally's
Umbrella

"Sally!" called her mother. "I want you to go to the newspaper shop for me and fetch me my magazine."

"Must I?" called back Sally. "It looks as if it's going to pour with rain, Mummy."

"Well, take your umbrella, then," said her mother. "I gave you a lovely one for your birthday. You ought to be pleased to use it."

"Mummy, my shoes let in the wet," said Sally, trying to think of another excuse not to go.

"Well, put on your wellington boots, then, if your shoes want mending," said Mother. "Here's a pound. Now you go along at once, before the shop shuts. Your umbrella and your boots are in the hall cupboard. Hurry, Sally."

Sally took the pound. Bother! Now she would have to go – and she did so badly want to finish her book.

She put on her boots. She put on her coat. She took her umbrella. She held the pound in her hand and she set off.

Well, it began to pour with rain, just as Sally had thought it would. How it pelted down! She put up her umbrella and trotted down the road, hoping there would soon be puddles she could splash through. Her mother didn't mind her doing that if she had her boots on.

The rain stopped very suddenly. Sally put down her umbrella. She came to the newspaper shop and walked in.

"Can I have Mummy's magazine, please?" she said. But when she wanted to pay for it the pound wasn't in her hand. It was gone.

"Oh, dear – I must have dropped it," said Sally, and back she went, hunting along the road for the pound. But it was quite gone.

She went home, upset. "I've lost the money, Mummy," she said. "I'm so sorry. I didn't hear it drop or I would have known I'd lost it. I can't imagine where it is!"

"That's careless of you, Sally," said her mother. "Here's another pound. Now don't you dare to come back and say you've lost that one, too!"

"Of course not," said Sally, and she set off again, holding the money tightly in her hand, and the umbrella in the other. It wasn't raining any more, so she didn't need to have it up this time.

She splashed through a puddle and

made such a shower of drops that some went down into her boots. "Oh, dear," she said, and looked to see if her socks were wet. They didn't seem to be. She walked on to the shop – and would you believe it, when she got there, she hadn't got the pound again! She stared at her empty hand in dismay.

"Well! Your mother won't be at all pleased with you!" said the shopkeeper, and put the magazine back on the shelf again.

Sally nearly cried. This was most mysterious. Another pound gone! Well, she must have dropped it by that big puddle she splashed through. That's where it must have gone.

So back she went to the puddle. She looked into it. She looked all round it. She looked in the road and by the side of the road. No pound.

"Bother! Somebody must have come by and picked it up," said poor Sally, and went home very slowly indeed, afraid that Mother would be crosser than ever.

But she wasn't. She was sorry to see

Sally's frightened, upset little face. She patted her.

"Never mind! It was my fault for sending you shopping with money. You're too little to take care of it yet."

"I'm not, really," Sally said in a small voice. "I kept them both carefully – and then they just disappeared. I'm sure I didn't drop them. I would have heard them if I had. It must be a magic spell, Mummy."

"In that case, they'll probably come back again," said Mother. "We'll hope so, anyway! Now put your coat on again, because Granny has just phoned to say will we go and have lunch with her today. We'll go now."

Well, that was nice. It was always fun to go to Granny's. Sally set off with her mother, carrying her umbrella in case it rained again. But it didn't.

They got to Granny's. She was at the front door, waiting for them. She smiled when she saw them.

"Well, well, here's little Sally with her new umbrella!" she said. "Let's have a look at it, Sally!" She took it and opened it – and, dear me, down on the top of Granny's head fell a pound. She was most surprised.

"Oh!" squealed Sally. "There's one of the pounds, Mummy. It was down the umbrella! Oh, I'm so glad!"

"Well, now perhaps the other will turn up," said her mother, laughing. "Come along, we must go in."

"Take off your boots first, Sally," said Granny. "Shall I pull them off for you?" She pulled one boot off – and then the other. And out of the second one shot – a pound!

"Well, goodness gracious, child, are you made of pounds?" cried Granny.

"Mummy! Mummy! The other pound was in my boot!" squealed Sally. "I didn't lose that one either."

Well, wasn't that peculiar? Sally couldn't help thinking that there might be some magic about. One pound in her umbrella, and the other in her boots – very strange.

And would you believe it, when she got home she felt in her pocket – and there was another pound there, too! That was very extraordinary, because Sally knew she had only had her hanky there when she set out to Granny's.

"There *is* magic about," she said, happily. "So you can't blame me for losing pounds any more, Mummy. I can't help it if there's magic about."

But I shouldn't be surprised if Granny had popped that pound in her pocket for a surprise, would you? It's the sort of thing grannies do – the nice ones, anyway!

The Little Blue Boat

The little blue boat lay in the corner of the shop window. It was called *Saucy Sue* and it had two tiny oars.

"I'll buy that boat for Billy," said Mother and she went into the shop. "He told me he badly wanted a boat!" So she bought the little *Saucy Sue* and took it home to Billy.

But Billy didn't like it. "Oh, Mummy!" he said. "What a silly little boat! I want a steamer or a battleship – not a stupid little boat like that."

"It's a dear little boat," said his mother. But Billy turned up his nose at it. The boat was sad. It knew it was small, but it couldn't help that. It badly wanted to be floated on water, but Billy wasn't going to bother to do that!

"Stupid boat!" he said, and threw it out in the garden! He wouldn't even put it into his toy cupboard. He didn't want it. He was a spoilt and silly little boy.

The boat lay out there on the garden path. Sooner or later someone would come along and tread on it. The boat dreaded that. It would be terrible to be broken to bits before it had even felt water beneath it. All boats long for water, and this little blue boat wanted it too.

Billy forgot all about it. The sun shone down and blistered the paint. A mouse ran off with one of the oars. A beetle ran up the other one, and it fell out of the boat.

Then the rain came and washed all the blue paint off the boat. "You are an ugly old boat, aren't you?" said the mouse, coming back.

"I'm not old. I'm really quite new," said the boat sadly. "This rain has washed all my paint away."

The rain went on and on. A big puddle came round the boat. It liked the feel of it. Then the puddle got so deep that the

boat found itself floating! How happy it was!

"I'm on water. I'm floating!" said the boat, and enjoyed the tiny waves on the puddle.

The puddle grew bigger. The garden path was flooded. The little boat floated down it, just as if it was floating down a stream!

The flooded garden was silvery with water. At the bottom was a real stream, and the water ran into it, carrying the boat with it. Soon it was sailing down the stream, as happy as could be!

It floated on and on. The rain stopped

and the sun came out. But still the little boat floated on. It liked the feel of the water below it.

But soon it felt lonely. There had been so many toys to talk to in the toyshop. Now there was nobody at all. The fishes didn't speak a word to the boat. The water-beetles were afraid of it.

"I wish that boy Billy had been kind to me!" thought the little boat, as it floated down the stream. "I could have had fine games with him."

The stream came to a duck-pond. It flowed through this, and out at the other side. But the boat didn't go with it, for a duck saw it and pounced on it.

It carried the boat to the side of the pond. Then it found that it could not eat it and threw it on the bank.

"What has that duck got?" said a little girl's voice, and she came running up. "Oh, look – it's a tiny boat. What a dear little boat! Mummy, I haven't got a boat. Can I have this one?"

"Well, we shall never know who it belongs to, so I think you can have it,"

144

said her mother, and the little girl picked it up joyfully.

"All its paint has been washed off and it hasn't got a name or oars," she said. "But I don't mind. It's a dear little boat."

"Daddy will give it a coat of paint for you," said her mother. "We'll take it home."

So the little girl carried the boat home and her father painted it red for her. It looked very smart. "I will paint a name on it for you," said Father. "We will give it your own name, Susan. We will call it *Saucy Sue!*"

That was odd, wasn't it, because that was the name the boat had had before. It was glad it didn't have a new name.

"It looks lovely now," said Susan. "I shall sail it in my bath every night. It shall live in the bathroom soap-rack with my duck and my goldfish, and I shall make it swim with them."

So it did, every night, and it was very happy indeed. Now it had three friends – Susan, the duck and the goldfish, and it liked them all. It loved floating in the warm bath water too.

One day a little boy came to spend the

day and night with Susan. His name was Billy – and yes, he was the very same Billy who had first had the boat, and thrown it away!

He and Susan had a bath together at night, and she put the duck, the goldfish and the boat into the water. The little red boat floated beautifully.

Billy loved it. "I like your boat," he said. "It's called *Saucy Sue*, and it's like a boat I once had, but mine was blue. Will you give me your boat?"

"No," said Susan. "I love it. It's mine. It floats in the bath with me every night."

The boat wouldn't float near Billy. It didn't like him. It kept behind Susan's pink back. Billy was sad when he went to bed, because he did so badly want the little red boat, and Susan wouldn't give it to him.

I'm glad she didn't, aren't you? She still has it, and when I see her in her bath, I see the *Saucy Sue* too. It still floats beautifully, and bobs up and down just like a real boat. It was lucky to come to Susan, wasn't it?

Mr Tantrum
and the Fog

Mr Tantrum was a bad-tempered fellow and nobody in Heigh-Ho Village liked him at all. He was always frowning, he hardly ever spoke without shouting, and he flew into a temper about just nothing at all!

The worst of it was that everyone was afraid of him. The children were frightened of being chased by him. The shopkeepers hated his loud voice and haughty ways. The ordinary village folk disliked to see him coming along to talk to them because he always disagreed with everything they said, and was most rude about it.

Mr Tantrum had plenty of money and he did what he liked, said what he liked, and never cared twopence about anybody else. Nobody dared to stand up to him at all.

Only little Jiminy Jinks really said out loud what he thought of Mr Tantrum.

"If I were as big as he is I'd pull his hair and shout at him and give him a good slapping!" said Jiminy.

"Oh no, you wouldn't!" said the villagers. "You only say that because you are small and know that you will never have a chance to go for him. Don't boast. If you feel so badly about him, think of some idea to pay him out for his annoying ways!"

Jiminy went red. He didn't like being told that he boasted. He thought he would try and think of some way to punish Mr Tantrum, but although he thought for a long time he just couldn't find any way of teaching him a lesson.

It was the big fog that really put an idea into his head. Yes – he really did think of a marvellous idea!

"I know that Mr Tantrum is going to see his Aunt Jemima tomorrow evening," he thought. "And I know that he always finds it difficult to find his way back when he gets to the crossroads. I'll be waiting there for him – and I'll give him a little shock!"

Well, little Jiminy Jinks did a few extraordinary things before he went to meet Mr Tantrum at the crossroads. In the thick fog he went to where a big scarlet pillar box stood at the corner of the street. He took with him a large football, a big hat, a pot of glue, and a large old mackintosh.

Jiminy stuck the football on the top of the pillar box with glue. He put the hat

on it. That made it look exactly as if the pillar box had a head!

Then he wrapped the enormous old mackintosh round the pillar box and buttoned it up. It was a very tight fit.

Jiminy did giggle when he saw what the pillar box looked like in the fog.

"It looks exactly like a big, burly man," said Jiminy with a chuckle. "My word, Mr Tantrum will be sorry if he tries to fight Mr Pillar Box! Well – we'll see!"

Jiminy went off to the crossroads to meet Mr Tantrum. Soon he heard him coming along. Mr Tantrum stopped at the crossroads and Jiminy walked nearby.

"Hi! You there! Which is the way to Cherry Tree Street?" shouted Mr Tantrum in his most commanding voice.

"Oh, to your left there and straight on," said Jiminy. Now this certainly wasn't the quickest way to go – but Jiminy had a reason for sending him wrong, as we know.

Off went Mr Tantrum, without a word of thanks! Pretty soon he knew that he had gone wrong, and he looked about

151

for somebody else to ask the right way.

Jiminy had known he would do that! There was the pillar box, looming up just nearby, looking exactly like a big man! Mr Tantrum shouted to him.

"Hi, you! I want the way to Cherry Tree Street."

Now Jiminy had darted round the streets another way and had come up behind the pillar box. So he answered at once, in as deep a voice as he could make.

"Well, if you want the way, get it. Nobody is stopping you!"

Mr Tantrum was simply amazed to have such a rude answer.

"Look here!" he said in a loud voice. "I don't think you know who you're talking to."

"Well, by the sound of you I should think I must be talking to Mr Bad-Temper or Mr Very-Rude!" answered Jiminy, who was thoroughly enjoying himself.

Mr Tantrum was so angry that he almost choked.

"I suppose you think that because

you're a big fat fellow you can treat
people how you like!" he shouted.

"No, no," answered the pillar box. "It's
you who think that, dear Mr Furious.
Everyone in the village knows how you
behave, just because you're a big, rich,
bad-tempered fellow! Ah, you'd behave
very differently if you were small and
poor."

"Now look here, if you dare to say
another word to me, I'll punch you!"
cried Mr Tantrum, so angry that he

almost swallowed his tongue.

"I'll speak lots more words!" shouted the pillar box. "I'll tell you all about yourself! About your bad manners, your disagreeable ways, your loud voice, and your bad tempers. I'll . . ."

But that was just too much for Mr Tantrum! He quite lost his temper and he struck out at the pillar box in a great rage. His hand hit against the hard metal side of the pillar box and Mr Tantrum yelled with pain. He danced about holding his hand. Jiminy darted out from behind the pillar box and knocked off Mr Tantrum's hat.

Mr Tantrum thought that the pillar box had done it, of course.

He rushed at it again, shouting, "I'll teach you to knock off my hat! Just wait till you feel both my fists!"

The pillar box waited. It didn't mind at all! *Slap! Bang!* Mr Tantrum went for that pillar box with both his fists, and good gracious me, how he hurt himself!

"Come on again!" yelled Jiminy, from behind the box. "Come on! I don't care

how hard you hit me. Kick me if you like!"

Well, then Mr Tantrum went quite mad, and he rushed once more at the pillar box and hit out and kicked with all his might. He nearly broke his fingers, he nearly broke his toes! How he hurt himself!

And last of all he hit out at the football head on top of the pillar box and sent it flying off into the fog. That surprised Mr Tantrum very much, and gave him a real shock. He stood still and stared. He had meant to hurt this fat rude man, but he really hadn't meant to knock off his head. He was frightened.

Jiminy came up to him. "Hello, Mr Tantrum," he said. "What's happening here?"

"N-n-n-nothing," answered Mr Tantrum nervously, holding his hands against his chest, for they hurt him very much.

"Mr Tantrum! You've knocked this poor fellow's head right off!" cried Jiminy. "See what your bad temper has led you

to! We always said you would do
something dreadful if you didn't try to
manage your temper! How could you
knock somebody's head off? I must fetch
a policeman."

"No, no – don't do that!" begged Mr
Tantrum, shivering like a jelly. "Please
don't. I'm very sorry, really I am. Don't
tell anybody."

"I must certainly go and fetch a
policeman," said Jiminy in a very solemn
voice. "We can't have you going about
doing things like this."

He disappeared a little way into the

fog. Soon he heard the sound of running feet. Mr Tantrum was rushing away before the policeman came! Jiminy went back to the big pillar box, leaned against it, and laughed till the tears ran down his cheeks!

Then he found the football head and the hat, unbuttoned the mackintosh, and went home. In the morning he went round to everyone's house and told them about the joke he had played on Mr Tantrum. How they laughed!

"We'll see whether he is quite so tiresome as usual!" they said. So they waited for Mr Tantrum to come to market to do his shopping.

But he didn't come! He had packed his bag, caught the earliest bus, and gone to his Aunt Jemima. He didn't come back again, but people who met him said that he was quite, quite different. In fact, he is now known as Mr Meek-and-Mild, so you can tell that he learned his lesson all right. Poor Mr Tantrum!

Mr Stamp-About
and Bellow the Brownie

"Here comes Bellow the brownie," said Tippy to Winks. "Let's eat our apples quickly or he'll take them from us!"

Bellow saw them gobbling their apples and he yelled at them. "Hey! Where did you get those apples?"

"Off a tree at home," said Tippy.

Bellow caught him by the shoulder. "Have you got any more apples on you?" he said. "Turn out your pockets. Ha – empty! Well, lead me to this tree and I'll help myself."

"No, please don't. You'd take so many," said Winks. "Let Tippy go."

Bellow caught hold of Winks, too, and he shook them both very roughly.

"Lead me to this tree!" he said in his loud voice. "Quick march, both of you!"

"This way," said Tippy meekly, and walked off to the left, with Bellow still holding him fast. Winks looked at Tippy, surprised to think that he was going to lead Bellow to their precious apple-tree. Tippy winked at him, which surprised Winks even more.

Down the street they went, and up the hill. Down the hill and over a field. Bellow shouted in their ears. "Go quicker! I want those apples!"

So Winks and Tippy began to trot. Tippy panted loudly, and Bellow grinned. He liked catching people and making them run!

"Where's this apple-tree?" he shouted. "We ought to be nearly there."

"Not far away now," panted Tippy, and he pointed to a little house on a hill. "Soon be there!"

Winks looked at him in surprise. What was Tippy up to? That wasn't their house. It belonged to Mr Stamp-About!

They came to the gate. Bellow let go of their arms and Tippy sank down on the wall, pretending to pant heavily.

"Where's this tree?" demanded Bellow, looking into the front garden. "I can't see it."

"Go round the back," panted Tippy. "I'm so out of breath I can't walk a step farther. If there are no apples on the ground, climb the tree!"

Bellow went round to the back of the little house. Ah – there was the apple tree – but only one or two apples lay on the ground. He would climb it and stuff his pockets full.

Up the tree he went. What lovely apples! He would pick as many as he

pleased – and he'd come back tomorrow and the next day, too, if he wanted to.

Tippy tiptoed round the house and looked to see what Bellow was doing. Good – he was up the tree! He went back and whispered to Winks, and they both tiptoed up the garden path to the front door. They knocked quietly.

The door was flung open and Mr Stamp-About stood there, frowning and glaring. "What do you want to come and disturb me for in the middle of my afternoon nap?" he shouted.

"Please, Mr Stamp-About, there's somebody up your apple-tree," said Tippy.

Mr Stamp-About gave a roar that sounded just like one of Bellow's and rushed round the house at once, almost knocking Tippy and Winks over. They followed him to the corner of the house and peeped round it.

Mr Stamp-About was thunderstruck to see Bellow up his apple-tree, picking apples and stuffing them into his pockets! He gave such a yell that Bellow almost fell out of the tree in fright.

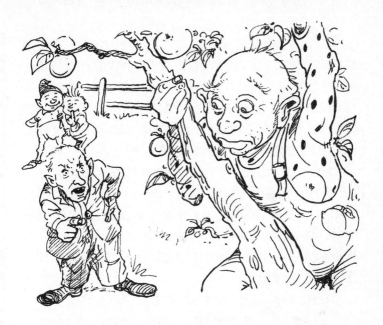

"HEY! YOU UP THERE! What do you think you're DOING?" yelled Stamp-About.

Bellow was astonished to see a very angry man stamping about below the tree, glaring up at him.

"Who are you?" he said.

"What does that matter? You're up my tree, stealing my apples! What's your name?" shouted Stamp-About.

"This isn't your tree. It belongs to Tippy and Winks," said Bellow, scared.

"Ho, it does, does it? Then how was it that Tippy and Winks came to tell me there was a thief up my apple-tree?" roared Stamp-About. "You come on down! You let me show you what happens to thieves in my apple-tree!"

Bellow didn't want to come down. He felt much safer up the tree, and he really couldn't understand this at all. Tippy and Winks had certainly brought him here – so how could it be Mr Stamp-About's tree?

"I'm not coming down," he said.

"Then I'll come up after you and throw you down!" said Stamp-About, reaching for a low branch.

"No, no! I'll come down, I'll come down!" bellowed poor Bellow, hoping that he could jump from the lowest bough and run.

But Stamp-About was waiting for him – and what a time Bellow had! Stamp-About chased him all over the garden.

Tippy and Winks laughed and laughed. Stamp-About caught Bellow and made him empty his pockets. Then he gave

him a good shake and poor Bellow went racing up the lane, bellowing at the top of his voice.

Stamp-About felt pleased with himself. He saw Tippy and Winks creeping up behind him, watching Bellows run away.

"Hey, you," he said. "Thanks for telling me about that rascal. You can help yourself to all the apples I made him turn out of his pockets!"

"Oh, thank you, Mr Stamp-About," said Tippy. "We've a tree at home but it's only got a few apples on it. We shall be very glad of these!"

Off they went, their pockets full. They nibbled an apple each, feeling very pleased. "You were clever, Tippy," said Winks. "Very clever indeed."

"Look – there's Bellow," said Tippy, suddenly. "Shall we run away?"

"No. He won't want to take these apples!" said Winks. "He'll be afraid."

Winks was right. Bellow slunk by them like a dog with his tail down. He wasn't going to try any funny tricks with Tippy and Winks again. Why, they might lead him to a giant the next time – poor Bellow!

The Dancing Mouse's Key

The children were playing out in the fields. They had a ball, a doll's pram, and a mouse who danced round and round when he was wound up.

The mouse belonged to Robin. He was very proud of his dancing mouse, and wound him up a hundred times a day to show the others how he danced.

Everyone was excited that morning. It was Saturday, and a circus had come to the field beyond Farmer Lane's farm. The children were going to it that afternoon, and how they longed for the time to come!

"There is a really exciting trapeze act," said Katie.

"And a man that can walk the tight-rope!" said Bobby.

"And a big trampoline," said Lucy.

"And eight dancing horses!" said Harry.

"But I'm sure they won't dance as well as my micky-mouse!" said Robin, winding him up again, and making him dance in the grass.

"You and your micky-mouse!" said Katie. "I wonder you don't wear that key out, winding him up so much!"

Robin put the key into his pocket. He was sure it wouldn't wear out. Keys never did. He watched his little mouse dancing, and then he went to see an ant-hill that Harry had found. They watched the busy little ants for a long time, and then Bobby looked at his watch. He was very proud of it, for it always told the right time.

"Half past two," he said. "It's time we all went home and got ready for the circus. Come along!"

"I must wind up my micky-mouse to dance one more time," said Robin, and he felt in his pocket for the key.

It wasn't there! He felt a hole in his pocket – and he knew that the key must

have dropped out of it. Now his dancing mouse wouldn't be able to dance any more!

Robin was only six, and he was dreadfully upset. He opened his mouth and howled. Lucy ran up to him, thinking that he had hurt himself.

"I've lost Micky's key! I've lost Micky's key!" wept Robin. "I won't go home till I've found it."

"But you must," said Lucy. "Why, it's almost time to set off for the circus, Robin – and you must wash your face and hands first, and let your mother brush your hair."

"I won't go to the circus," wept Robin. "I'll stay here all afternoon by myself and look for Micky's key."

"You're silly, Robin," said Harry. "Come on, everyone. Leave Robin. He'll come along soon enough when he finds we're gone."

So Harry, Bobby and Katie ran off, but Lucy didn't really like to leave poor Robin when he was so unhappy. She was a kind little girl.

"Don't cry any more, Robin," she said. "I'll help you find your key. Hurry up and look with me."

So the two of them began to hunt in the grass, but, dear me, it seemed as if that key was nowhere to be found! Lucy began to be worried for the time was slipping on and she knew that she couldn't go to the circus if she was much later.

"Robin, let's go now," she said. "Come along. We shall be too late for the circus in a minute."

But Robin wouldn't go. He stood there, clutching his dancing mouse in one hand and wiping his eyes with the other. He didn't care about anything except finding his lost key.

"Oh, well," said Lucy. "If you won't come I'll stay with you – but I do hope we find the key soon!"

In a little while the other children ran out of their houses down the lane, waved to Lucy, and went off to the circus. Tears came into the little girl's eyes. Now she was too late to go. She went down on her hands and knees again and looked carefully for that missing key.

And what do you think she found? She found a four-leaved clover! Now, as you know, a four-leaved clover is supposed to be very lucky indeed, for it has magic in it! Lucy and the other children had often hunted for one and had never found one – and now here was a fine one, with four green leaves, a really-and-truly four-leaved clover!

"Look, Robin!" said Lucy joyfully. "I've found a four-leaved clover! Now I shall have some luck!"

"It's too late to be lucky," said Robin. "We've missed the circus now and haven't found my key."

"Why, here's the key, under this dandelion!" cried Lucy. And so it was! "My four-leaved clover has brought us luck already!"

"But it's too late for the circus," said Robin again.

"Hurry, and we'll see!" said Lucy. So they hurried. Robin went to his home and Lucy went to hers. It was too late for Lucy; but do you know, when Robin told his father how kind Lucy had been to him, he jumped up and said, "Well, that kind little girl won't miss the circus then! I'll get out the van and run both of you along to the circus straight away. Then you'll be in time."

So he got out the van in which he took his fruit to the market, called for Lucy, popped her in with Robin and tore down the lane to the circus. He paid for Lucy's ticket as well as Robin's, and they were given two good seats. They sat down just as the circus began! Wasn't that lucky?

It was a lovely circus, and when the circus people came in to give away balloons, who do you suppose got the

biggest? Yes, Lucy! And when the big clown went round shaking hands with the children, who do you suppose he gave a hug to? Yes, Lucy! Didn't she feel proud!

"My four-leaved clover really is bringing me luck," said the little girl happily. "I'm glad I stayed behind to help Robin."

On the way home Lucy found a pound lying on the path! Wasn't that good luck? And when she got home, there was her Uncle Jack, her very favourite uncle, come to take her out to tea with him in his car.

"Oh, Uncle Jack! This is all because of my four-leaved clover!" said Lucy happily. "Where are we going?"

"We're going to the town to have tea and ice creams," said Uncle Jack. "And then we're going to an old man I know who has a dear little puppy for sale, and I want to buy it for a nice little girl called Lucy."

"Uncle Jack!" squealed Lucy, who wanted a puppy more than anything else in the world. "Uncle Jack! You dear, kind uncle!"

Well, she had a lovely tea and two ice creams, and then they went to fetch the puppy. It was a little black spaniel with long drooping ears, the dearest little thing Lucy had ever seen.

"What will you call her?" asked Uncle Jack as they drove back in his car, with

Lucy cuddling the puppy, feeling very sleepy and very happy.

Lucy had a name for her, of course. Can you guess what it was? It was Clover! Lucy thought it would be such a lucky name.

Didn't she have a lot of luck? Do you want some as well? Well, just hunt about for a four-leaved clover and maybe you'll have some too.

He Lost
His Head!

Once upon a time there was a little fellow called Mr Fluster. Now, you may think that is a strange name, and so it is, but it suited him down to the ground.

You see, Mr Fluster was always losing his head about things, and getting into a terrible fluster. If anything unusual happened, or if he lost anything or got upset, he rushed here and there, untidied everything, and generally got into such a fluster that he made people most annoyed.

If he lost his collar stud he would begin to pull his hair and stamp about, and make his little wife very cross.

"Why lose your head about a silly little thing like a collar stud?" she would say. "Yesterday you got in a fluster because

177

your bus was five minutes late. And the day before; what an upset you were in just because the paper-boy left you the wrong paper. Really, Fluster, you should be ashamed of yourself."

Poor Mr Fluster! He was always losing his head about one thing and another and his wife really didn't know how to cure him. "You know, you're beginning to make me all hot and bothered and flustered, too, when things happen," she said. "Do stop it, Fluster."

But he couldn't seem to. He only got worse and worse, and one day, when he lost his purse, he was so upset that he quite lost his head, and ran after everyone to feel in their pockets. "Have

you taken my purse?" he cried. "Are you the person who's stolen it?"

Well, of course, you can't do things like that, and Mrs Fluster got very worried when she saw Mr Fluster behaving so stupidly.

"Pull yourself together!" she said sternly. "One of these days your head will come off and you really will lose it!"

But Mr Fluster didn't get any better at all, and at last Mrs Fluster went to see her old Great-aunt Goomy, who was a bit of a witch. They sat together in Aunt Goomy's kitchen and talked about Fluster.

"Can you tell me how to stop poor Fluster from losing his head about things a dozen times a day?" asked Mrs Fluster. "You're so very clever, Great-aunt."

Aunt Goomy's eyes twinkled. "What about giving him a fright, and making him really lose his head?" she said.

Mrs Fluster looked rather doubtful. "I'm not sure I would like Fluster without his head," she said.

"Ah, we won't take it off, or anything

like that," said Aunt Goomy, twinkling again. "No, no. But I could give you a spell that will make his head invisible as soon as he gets into a fluster. Then, when he looks into the glass, he'll not see his head, and he'll think he really has lost it!"

"Oh, that does seem a very good idea," said Mrs Fluster, and she twinkled too. "Yes, I'll try it. It will certainly give him a fright, and maybe stop his bad habits."

Aunt Goomy gave Mrs Fluster a box of fine powder. "You blow this lightly over the back of his head next time he gets into a fluster," she said. "It will make it quite invisible. All you have to do to make it come back again is to flap a duster at him."

"Thank you so much, Aunt Goomy," said Mrs Fluster, and took the powder home with her.

Now the next day Mrs Fluster had a little sewing-party. Five of her friends were to come, and, to keep Mr Fluster company, his friend Mr Flare-Up was to come to tea, too.

It was rather a pity that Mr Fluster had a friend like Mr Flare-Up, because Flare-Up had a hot temper and often upset Mr Fluster. Still, Mrs Fluster hoped things would be all right.

All her friends came to the sewing-meeting. Mr Fluster and Mr Flare-Up went to sit in the other room to talk and smoke. And very soon Flare-Up said something to upset Mr Fluster.

"Did you know that some bad boys have broken your fence at the bottom of your garden?" he began. "I saw them smashing it yesterday."

"Well, why didn't you stop them?" cried Mr Fluster. "My perfectly good fence! Oh, I'll punish those boys. No. I'll ring up the police. No, I'll go down to the fence this very minute and make you help me to mend it. Oh, what shall I do? What a state the world is in if boys can come and smash down fences!"

"Now, don't get in a fluster," said Flare-Up. "That's just silly and you know it. Keep your head – don't lose it over a stupid thing like that."

"You call that a stupid thing," cried Fluster, beginning to tear his hair. "Why, that fence cost me . . ."

Mrs Fluster heard the upset from the next room. She picked up the box of powder and went quietly into the room where Fluster and Flare-Up were shouting at one another. She opened the box and blew the fine powder all over the back of Fluster's head. Neither he nor Flare-Up saw what she did. Then she went quietly back into the other room, for she knew the spell would take a few minutes to act.

It acted very well! The magic powder began to make Fluster's head quite invisible. The top of it went first, then the middle of it, then the bottom part. Flare-Up stared at his friend in horror. Why, he hadn't got a head!

But he still had a voice. "What are you staring at me like that for?" cried Fluster. "What's the matter?"

"Oh, Fluster, you've lost your head," wailed Flare-Up. "Your wife always said you would, and now you have. It isn't there."

"Of course it's there!" yelled Fluster. "How could I talk or see if I hadn't got a head? I'm talking, aren't I? And I can see you and hear you. Well, of course I've got a head."

"You haven't, you haven't. You've lost it," said Flare-Up, beginning to feel frightened. It was horrid to see Fluster ending at his collar.

Fluster strode over to the big mirror and looked at himself. Then he felt himself go cold. He began to tremble. He saw himself in the mirror – but without a head. Yes, he certainly hadn't any head at all. Fluster simply couldn't believe it.

He ran into the other room, calling for his wife. Everyone looked up.

Mrs Thimble gave a scream. "Oh! The man's lost his head. Where's it gone?"

Mrs Needles jumped up in horror. "Oh, what's this? Where's your head gone, Fluster? Surely you haven't lost it?"

Mrs Fluster knew what had happened, of course, but she wasn't going to say a word. The others turned to her in amazement and fear.

"Fanny Fluster! Look what's happened to your poor husband. He's lost his head."

"That's nothing new," said Mrs Fluster, snipping away with her scissors. "He's always losing it about something or other. I told him one day it would go properly. And now it has. He's certainly lost it."

"Oh, Fanny, Fanny, what shall I do?" wailed poor Fluster. "I looked in the glass, and I hadn't a head. But I can talk and see, you know. Oh, oh, this is the most awful thing that has happened to me."

"It's no use telling him to keep his head about it, because he hasn't one," said Flare-Up, coming into the room and staring at Fluster. "Well, well, I've often heard people talk of others losing their heads, but I never thought I'd see it happen. He'd better see the doctor, hadn't he, Mrs Fluster?"

"Yes, yes, I'll go straight away and see the doctor," cried poor Fluster, and he raced out of the house. He bumped into the postman, and the man dropped all his letters and tore down the street in fright as soon as he saw Fluster without a head.

Everyone ran when they saw Fluster. Even the dogs barked and fled. He really was a most peculiar sight. He came to the doctor's at last, and rang the bell.

"Doctor, oh Doctor, I've lost my head!" he cried, when the door opened. But the doctor slammed it shut again. He was

186

most alarmed. He wasn't going to have people without heads walking into his house. He didn't know what to do for them, that was certain.

Fluster went home again, making such a noise of weeping and howling that everyone looked out to see what it was. And their eyes nearly fell out of their heads when they saw poor Fluster, and heard him talking with a mouth that wasn't there, and weeping tears from eyes that weren't there either.

There was no one at home but Mrs Fluster, still calmly sewing. Everyone else had gone, for they really felt too upset to stay. Fluster stared at his little wife.

"You don't seem at all upset about this," he said.

"Well, I don't see any reason to lose my head about it," said Mrs Fluster. "One person losing his head is quite enough. These things may be catching. I'm going to keep calm and quiet. You'd better, too. I'm sure it's the only way to find your head again, Fluster."

"I'll try. I really will try," said poor Fluster, and he sat down and tried to be calm. But it was very, very difficult.

"If only my head would come back again I'd be very, very careful never to lose it any more," he said, looking at himself in the mirror, and shivering to see how strange he looked.

"Nonsense, Fluster. You know you would straightway go and get upset about something and lose your head again," said Mrs Fluster, beginning to sew a very neat buttonhole. Fluster watched her.

"If you reminded me that my head might go when I get into a fluster it would stop me," he said.

"Do you think it would?" said Mrs Fluster, and she got up. She took a duster and walked behind poor Fluster.

"Yes, I know it would," groaned Fluster, putting his invisible head into his hands, and wondering why it felt as if he had one when the mirror told him he hadn't.

Mrs Fluster flapped her feather duster at the back of Fluster's head. Then she

went and sat down again. Fluster's head began to come back slowly. The chin came first. Mrs Fluster watched with great interest.

Fluster looked at himself in the glass. Then he looked again. He jumped up.

"Fanny!" he cried, "I believe my head is coming back. Look, isn't that my chin?"

"Yes. And there's your nose," said Mrs Fluster. "And your eyes, look. Oh good, you look much better now. And there's your hair coming back, too."

"Oh, thank goodness, thank goodness!" cried Mr Fluster, and he did a little dance round the table. "Oh, I thought I'd have to go for the rest of my life without my head. Oh, Fanny, I'll never, never lose it again."

"Well, mind you don't!" said Mrs Fluster; and she turned away to hide a smile. "It's a most unpleasant thing for everybody."

And now, when little Mr Fluster begins to get upset about things and go all hot and bothered, Mrs Fluster speaks to him sternly.

"Fluster," she says, "keep your head. Don't lose it. When annoying or unusual things happen, keep your head. You may want to use it. Remember what happened to you once, Fluster – and keep your head!"

Well, he's much better now, but it must have been a funny sight to see him lose his head properly, musn't it? Do you ever lose yours? I hope not.